NO SUCH THING AS

PERFECT

SARAH DALTRY

Also by Sarah Daltry

Dust

Backward Compatible: A Geek Love Story

The Love Song of J. Alfred Prufrock

Bitter Fruits

"Sometimes one is guided by what they say of themselves, and very frequently by what other people say of them, without giving oneself time to deliberate and judge."

– Jane Austen

PART I:

FALLING

1.

"My name's Lily and James Naismith ruined high school for me," I offer.

It's too hot in this room. The window fan is just blowing more heat over us, along with some old dust or dirt from the window. It makes the noise of plastic that is being asked to do more than plastic can do; the fan's cheapness makes it too weak to be a fan and it groans with its own failure.

I'm not good at social events; I never have the right thing to say. This is some kind of floor meeting for all new students and I'm sitting in the middle of my RA's room with ten other girls, all of us in pajama pants, and I'm trying to sound interesting.

"I mean, he didn't personally. I think he died almost a hundred years ago," I stutter.

"So why don't you explain how the inventor of basketball *did* ruin high school then?" one girl asks. She's angry, but I don't know her. I don't know anyone, except my roommate Kristen, and so far all I know about her is that she's majoring in education, she brought the fridge, and she's decorated her side of our dorm room to look like the inside of a Pepto-Bismol bottle.

This girl doesn't want to hear my story. She doesn't want to be here. I don't, either, but now that I'm here, I was the one dumb enough to open my mouth.

"It was gym class," I try to explain. "I don't know. Something about ed reform. We had homework and tests and all that in gym now and I'd been up all night writing an essay about James Naismith. I hadn't slept and I was in a rush trying to make the bus that morning."

It had been cold, the rushing towards winter that mirrors the years that aren't like this one. This is one where summer lingers and it resists every attempt to make it yield to fall. I remember the leaves were already falling that year, even though it was only early

September. Some years it seemed like they were in a greater rush to die. In the moments between life, each leaf took its suicidal leap and fell slowly while no one noticed. We only notice when they're all dead and suddenly the sky hangs on us and we crave shade.

The bus was about to pull away from the curb near my house and I cried out for it, running faster and slipping on a clump of leaves. The entire patch was squishy. I wondered as I fell if I had taken out a small family of worms. My outfit was ruined, but it wasn't the clothes that scared me...

"I tripped on leaves and fell on the driveway hard. The gravel left a slash along my cheek and it looked like someone had punched me. That was the day of school pictures, which we used for the yearbook and our IDs. Not to mention the fact that my mom..."

I can't finish. I don't want to talk about my mother. I certainly don't feel like confiding in these girls, don't feel like telling them how disappointed she was, don't want to confess that I ruined everything. It wasn't my fault that fall had come early, but I ruined the pictures and in her album of school photos, my freshman year still remains a giant, empty black page. A constant

3

reminder that I will never be whole, never be perfect, never be what she wanted.

"What about your mom?" someone else asks. They don't care about this story. They don't care about me. Everyone is only politely listening because we were promised ice cream for showing up, although it's mandatory.

"Nothing."

I don't want to tell my story anymore. I want the fan to stop trying. I want it to be tomorrow and the day after and any day when I can start in the morning and get through to night without making a mistake.

It's dropped, though, anyway, because Ellie, the RA, turns to another girl, who is pocketing a handful of condoms. "You don't need to take them all," she barks. "I have plenty, but other people practice safe sex, too. Unless you're planning on having a massive orgy tonight, you can probably come back and get some later."

The condom hoarder blushes and returns half her pile and the floor meeting turns back to pointless small talk and ice breakers that no one wants to be a part of. Ellie hands us soggy ice cream sandwiches for guessing each other's majors. The fan clicks another meaningless rotation.

I've been a college student for six hours now and I've never been so lonely in my entire life.

****

"Do you want to order a pizza?" Kristen asks an hour later in our room. I shouldn't begrudge her the fact that she's color coordinated her laptop, bedding, hangers, and lamp, since my side of the room is sporting the jailhouse chic look and I'm still living out of cardboard. I waited until the last day to move in, because I wasn't ready.

"I'm starving," I admit. "I would love that."

"Cool. I'll order. Do you want anything special?"

"Whatever you're having. Just tell me how much," I say.

When she goes to the lobby to get the menus and to see if anyone else on the floor wants food, I check my phone. My boyfriend, Derek, is moving into his dorm today and I haven't heard from him.

"Hey, Lily, this is Lyle," Kristen says when she returns, introducing the lanky guy following her into our room, carrying the menu. "And Don."

"Hey," I say.

"Lily's waiting for a call, I think," Kristen explains to them. "She keeps staring at her phone."

"Sorry, I..." I don't know what to tell them. That Derek's an hour away? That although my grades are better than his and this is a better school, I already miss him? That I regret trying to be independent and it's only been a day? How pathetic.

"Boyfriend," Lyle confirms. "Right?"

I nod. "I don't mean to be rude. I've just been waiting all day for him to call."

"Don't worry about it," Kristen says. "I'd probably be anxious, too." She opens the menu and takes out her phone. "So, two cheese and a pepperoni? You guys want fries?"

"Poppers," Lyle says. "I'll pay."

I just nod again. I wish I was better at socializing, but my only real friend, besides Derek, is my best friend, Abby and she's traveling in Europe so she can "find herself" before starting college. I'm stuck trying to figure this all out by myself.

Don's about to say something when my phone rings.

"Sorry. I just need to take this." I go into the hall, where I can be alone.

"Hey, sweetie. Settling in?" Derek asks.

"I miss you," I reply. "Is that dumb?"

"No, I miss you, too. But hell, we survived almost a year while you were still living at home. And now you won't have your parents telling you what to do all the time."

"It's kind of quiet here. It's not what I expected." Everyone's parents left hours ago and now there's just the lonely echo of the lives we're trying to leave behind us.

Derek laughs. "Give it time. It hasn't even been a full day. When do your classes start again?"

I've told him several times, because we waited to move in on the same day, although his classes don't start until next week. "Tomorrow," I remind him.

"Right. Well, you'll do fine. Call me tomorrow night after you get done with classes, okay?"

I want to ask him to stay on the phone, but I know he's probably trying to set up his room. He's probably hungry, too, and I should get back to my pizza. I feel the ache of needing to speak clutching at my throat,

7

but I swallow the words and hold them back. "I will," I say. "Say hi to Jon, okay?"

"I will. Love you," he says, but he hangs up before I can tell him that I love him, too.

It was raining on the day I fell in love with Derek. That's what I remember most. Everything was damp. It felt like the entire world had been soaked through, and it was way too cold for July.

We were camping, because my mother had watched Oprah or some talk show that suggested the best way to "connect with family" was to "break away from the ordinary." This was her year of connecting, because another show had said that's what good parents did. So thanks to Oprah, we were headed to the wilderness at the command of my mother, a woman who lives for Crock Pots, bath soaps, and electricity. I'd helped my parents and brother, Jon, along with his friend, Derek, load up our SUV and we sat on a crowded highway, waiting to engage with nature. Abby was supposed to come, but she'd gotten poison ivy a few days before we left and now she was at home, covered in Calamine lotion, texting me images of poison ivy plants so I didn't meet the same fate.

The wilderness, it turned out, was only ninety minutes away in a resort town in New Hampshire, and our tent was pitched less than thirty yards from the cabin my parents had rented "just in case." A cabin with an oven, TV reception, and Wi-Fi. It took only six hours before my mom decided she preferred the comforts of indoor life to the bugs and trees after all. This left me to spend the first night in the tent with my dad, Jon, and Derek. It was leaning precariously towards the west. I knew it was west, because the only use I got from the compass I bought for our adventure was to gauge the leaning of the tent.

The next morning, before dawn, my dad woke us up, declaring that he and his back weren't cut out for the ground, before heading inside to the luxuries of a mattress as well. And then there were three.

By the time the storm hit on the third day and staying outdoors meant braving the elements, too, only

Derek and I were still up for eating food on sticks and sleeping in the dirt.

You have to understand - at fourteen, there was not much in the way of excitement in my life, so this little change was topping the charts. The tent was making its westward expansion, likely towards the river, and the wind was helping it along nicely. However, I was determined to stick it out, because I wanted something different in my life.

"Are you having fun?" Derek asked as the tent shook again.

"I am, actually," I admitted. "Is that weird?"

"I don't think so. It's like an adventure."

"Right?"

Oprah would have approved of our willingness to try something new, although we weren't exactly family. I'd always sort of thought of Derek as an extension of my brother, but then it rained and we were in a tent and the whole world was suddenly different. When he smiled at me, I noticed for the first time that his eyes got scrunchy and they almost sparkled a little. I also noticed that I wanted to look at his eyes more.

Until that afternoon, I had never been interested in guys. Abby would go on about some cute boy in a class or on TV, but I tended to focus on reading or anything that kept things from getting complicated. But when Derek smiled and his eyes did that funny thing, I wanted to be the reason he smiled.

"What's wrong?" he asked. "You're looking at me funny."

"Sorry. Nothing. I was thinking," I stammered.

"Okay, cool. Do you want to play cards or something?" He broke out the deck and started dealing without really getting a confirmation, but I did want to play cards. I suddenly wanted to do anything that would keep Derek looking at me.

I picked up my hand, which I had to peel from the canvas floor of tent. I didn't even know what game we were playing, but it didn't matter.

"You know that painting of the dogs playing poker?" I asked.

"Yeah. My uncle has that in his basement."

"Well, I feel like we're the dogs, except we're fish. You know, 'cause it's wet?"

Derek blinked, his eyes going out of focus, but then his smile grew wider. "You are really weird, Lily." He touched my arm when he said it and I knew he would never be just my brother's friend again.

As the afternoon turned to evening, the dark sky never changed. We spent hours playing cards, eating the snacks Jon had left behind and talking about school. Derek had just finished his freshman year, but high school was still only a vague concept for me. His braces made it hard for him to talk when he got excited, so sometimes he slurred random words. It was cute; a few months later, when he had his braces removed, I missed it.

Eventually my dad came to get us, because the weather wasn't going to let up. I wanted to text Abby, to tell her what I was feeling, but I didn't understand it and I didn't want to make it real. I didn't talk about it for month to anyone. Especially since Derek acted as if the day we'd spent meant nothing during the rest of the trip, and maybe it had. Maybe it was only me who felt something different that afternoon.

We spent the last night as a group around the campfire and I kept trying to recreate the smile and the feeling I'd had with Derek just a few days before, but he didn't look at me at all. I would spend three years of high school trying to relive that rainy afternoon in the tent, but Derek went on to become popular and everything I wasn't. Meanwhile, I studied and I got good grades and maybe I was pretty, but it didn't matter, because I only wanted him to pay attention. But no matter how much I wanted it, he never did.

My life from there forward stayed on track, following the plan and schedule, but sometimes, in the late hours when everyone was sleeping, I remembered what it felt like to be a girl who made a boy smile and a girl who stayed outside in the rain when everyone else took the easy way.

The college admissions essay question prompts you to talk about how you can bring something new to the school, but after sitting through a few classes, I start to wonder how many essays get read. I like to think that I'm more than a perfect GPA, plus a nicely varied combination of extracurriculars that included Student Council, track, and National Honor Society, as well as dance classes my mom thought I needed to take. However, the brochures sell diversity, while reality seems to be a collection of people as desperately hopeless as I am.

"Am I in the right place?" the guy sitting next to me in Literary Study asks. The classroom is small, nothing like those lecture halls they show in movies. There are about twelve old and hard wooden chairs around a table too big for discussion without shouting. The chalkboards on the walls look like they've never been used. It's warm in here, too, but the overhead fan is trying to stake its superiority to my RA's plastic one, blowing my notebook open but still not changing the temperature.

"Literary Study – Austen?" I answer. I adjust my backpack, which is on the table and too full. I bought all my books before my first class and I haven't had time to get back to my dorm yet.

"Shit. I thought it was Trig." He leaves and I'm sitting next to the only empty chair during the entirety of the class. I tell myself it's not a sign of things to come.

Fortunately, Elinor Dashwood is familiar. As soon as the professor says we're starting with *Sense and Sensibility*, I'm back to what I know. I understand Elinor and her responsibilities. I know about being reasonable. When my parents bought me a copy for Christmas during freshman year of high school, the book felt like punishment. Even the inscription – *A good start for your SAT reading and college goals* – was instruction, but I read it anyway, because it was a book and that's what my Friday nights consisted of usually. While Abby dated and broke up with guy after guy and while Jon and Derek partied, I sat at home and read and studied. But the Dashwoods became my friends. Who needed to come home smelling like beer when you could be out riding with any of Austen's heroes anyway?

I leave class planning our first assignment – a character study on one of the Dashwoods - and lost in the early 19th century. I yearn for the quiet simplicity of the stories.

"Hey, you dropped this."

I turn towards the voice. The guy holding my book, which I must have dropped while daydreaming of parties and piano fortes, reaches out to hand it me. His arm is circled by black lines, tattoos snaking under his sleeve. I take the book and look up, meeting his eyes.

"Thanks."

"Are you reading this?" he asks. Dark hair nearly covers his eyes, which are swirls of indigo, subtle seas of suspicion, broken with a tempest of playfulness.

"Well, technically. I mean, I've already read it several times, but yes, we are reading it for class."

17

"I personally always liked Marianne," he says.

"You've read it?"

"Is that surprising?"

"No, but slightly cliché. Is this the scene where we discover we knew each other as infants, too?" I ask.

He laughs. "I don't think so. I think it's just a pretty common book."

"Valid point. So why Marianne? Isn't she a little too... reckless?"

"Not at all. She's far more intriguing, don't you think? She knows what she wants, even when it's wrong for her. I bet Marianne would be a lot of fun."

I don't know why it feels like a challenge suddenly, but I tuck my book tighter into my bag and take a step back. "Her *fun*, as you call it," I argue, "almost ruins her. It's selfish and immature to think about nothing but one's own passions."

"I see. So I suppose I should call you Elinor, then?"

"You don't need to call me anything. Thanks for picking up my book."

"I'm Jack," he says. "Sorry if I upset you. I was just trying to help." The light in his blue eyes flashes out quickly, leaving a hollow darkness in its place. The sticky heat of a stubborn summer is drained from the world in the empty chill that enters his expression. I didn't intend to be mean. He was only making conversation.

"No, I mean, I'm sorry. You're right. Marianne's okay."

I watch him pause. I want to say something, to apologize for some reason, to try to shake the sudden guilt at the way he's staring at me. His look went from curiosity to anger and then to something else. I understand now what they mean about seeing yourself through someone else's eyes. He's reflecting everything I fear about myself in this look – and I hate it.

He takes out a pack of cigarettes and places one between his lips. "All right. See you around, Elinor."

"Wait," I plead, but he's gone.

"Awesome. You are already pissing people off," I mutter to myself.

I head to dinner, where I load my plate with pasta, focusing on food instead of feeling like I said something stupid. I'm sure he doesn't care anyway; it was just a dumb conversation.

Kristen is sitting with Lyle and Don and some of the girls I recognize from our floor. The condom hoarder is there, too. I wish I knew how people could walk into the unknown and just start new without caring. They're already acting like they've known each other for ages and I can't even remember anyone else's name. I promise myself I'll try harder. This is not supposed to be hard. I look around the cafeteria and everyone's talking and eating and settled. Classes just started but I'm the only person who seems out of place.

"Lily, what are you doing tonight?" Lyle asks. "Do you want to go to a party?"

"Oh, I don't know. I'm not really a party kind of person," I say.

"Come on, it'll be fun," Kristen says. "It's just a group of us and some guys from the other wing. Nothing crazy."

"I have a lot of homework already. Maybe this weekend?"

"Sure. If you change your mind, we're just down the hall," Lyle says. "410. Come on by. I'm sure we'll be up late, so even if you want to pop in after you finish your homework. It isn't going to get wild or anything. We'll probably just play Xbox."

"You really know how to woo girls, don't you?" Kristen teases.

"You're coming, aren't you?"

She blushes and looks away. It's amazing. It's so normal, so natural. How do people connect that quickly without trying?

"What's your major?" Don asks me, taking my attention away from Lyle and Kristen.

"English." I wait for the comments and questions. *Oh, so you want to be a teacher? What good is English? Really – you must like reading, then?* My mother's voice won't get out of my mind. I've been through the conversations for almost two years now; there is nothing worthwhile about living in make-believe. However, when I finally got on campus for orientation and was asked to officially declare a major, her voice screaming about practicality didn't stop me from writing the word on the paper. And once it was written, it had to be true.

"Oh my God, I know," one of the girls says. "I already have two papers due and two books to read.

What's that about? I thought English was supposed to be easy."

I shrug. "I don't mind. I like reading. I just figure I'll try to get the work done before doing anything else, though."

Everyone starts talking at once about their classes, which professors are insane, how much work they do or don't have, where there might be parties this weekend, and it's noisy and chaotic. I finish my pasta and no one notices when I gather my stuff and head out. The sun has already set and the walk back to my dorm is quiet.

I'm supposed to call Derek when I get in, and I wish I knew what to say. I want to tell him that today was great, that I'm already loving college, that I have the same confidence everyone around me seems to have. Again, I wonder if I should've gone to the same school as him, but we had countless conversations about what was best for my future. I know it's true, that I'll be better off here, but I feel like I'm just waiting to screw up. It's hard to think about the future when you can't get over the past.

All of the other kids were running through the field, chocolate smeared onto their clothes, desperate for more eggs. Jon was fighting with a boy from the next town over, but I couldn't hear what they were arguing about. It was probably candy anyway. No one seemed to notice or care. I thought about joining the rest of the kids, but my dress was pure white and the black patent leather Mary Janes had just been polished.

"You should go join them," my dad encouraged. "I hear the golden egg this year is extra special."

For nine years, my parents had brought Jon and me to the church Easter egg hunt in town. It was one of my earliest memories, even though I only remembered the last few. Jon, at eleven, cared less about the eggs than he did about the competition. I liked the eggs; I had spent the last week helping my mom color and design them for the hunt. For each egg you turned in, you were given a piece of chocolate, but it was only the golden egg that mattered.

"I'll get dirty," I told him.

"That's okay. Live a little." He laughed and I might have listened. I might have gone on and crawled through the grass, but my mom appeared before I could move.

"Lily, your bow is coming loose," she snapped, pulling me by the ponytail backwards on the picnic bench. "How do you manage to cause such a mess all the time?"

"You should let her participate," my dad said to my mom.

"I did. She helped me make the eggs."

"You know what I mean."

My mother finished straightening and tightening my bow and turned me to face her. "Is that what you want? Do you want to run around in the dirt like an animal?" I shook my head. She looked at my father. "You shouldn't encourage her."

"Jon's out there thinking he's in the Old West, ready to have a high noon showdown over a Snickers, but poor Lily-" he started.

"I don't want to play, Dad. It's okay. My dress is too pretty. We still have to go out for dinner," I reminded him. I knew my mom would be devastated if I ruined my outfit before dinner.

"It's not like it's mud wrestling," he mumbled, but he stopped pushing.

Kayla, one of the girls from my reading class, was wearing a pretty dark blue dress and skipping past the tree by the church buildings. Her dress was still clean, because it could hide any dirt or grass stains. I wished I'd worn something darker.

She leaned down and dug in the grass for a minute, before lifting the golden egg. "I got it!" she yelled and everyone stopped. Everyone except Jon and the other boy, because they were still rolling around in the grass. "I win! I win!"

Mrs. Hallomeyer, the CCD teacher, brought Kayla and the golden egg over towards the benches, where the adults – and I – were sitting. The rest of the kids followed, each disappointed about not winning, although the supply of conciliatory candy seemed to appease most of them. Eventually, even Jon and his foe joined us all while Mrs. Hallomeyer talked about Jesus and gratitude and something that was somehow connected to the egg. The whole time, I just stared at Kayla. She gripped the egg close to her and grinned at me. I knew what she was thinking, because I was thinking it, too.

Only a week earlier, our reading teacher, Miss Stephens, had announced the winner of the book contest. Each of us had been asked to read and write reports on as many books as we could during the previous quarter. For each book we finished, we received a star on a chart. It had been me and Kayla down to the end, but I beat her by two books. When Miss Stephens had announced it, Kayla started to cry and said I was a cheater and a liar and that I'd never read those books. She said I only cared about winning and that I read easy books. She said a lot of things, but Miss Stephens knew they were lies. Unfortunately, most of my classmates didn't care, because Kayla had a pool and she brought cookies every Friday because her mom *didn't work and everyone else started calling me a liar, too.*

I really wished I had gotten my dress dirty and beaten her to that stupid egg.

"That's good, right?" Derek asks. He's been talking about rugby, which is apparently his new hobby. It's been a day and a half and he's on the rugby team, while I still don't know where the health center is.

"It is. I mean, yeah, of course it is."

"What's wrong? You sound... different."

I shake my head, sighing. "It's nothing. It's stupid. I don't know." I lie back on my bed, staring at the ceiling. Kristen talked me into putting up glow-in-the-dark stars since I didn't even bring a poster. My side is basically a wall, except for the few photos I have of Derek and me. All my other photos are framed or pressed in albums in my parents' living room.

"Well, it's not nothing. Talk to me, sweetie."

"It's just… I mean, how do you…" I pause, reaching for the words. "You just always seem to know what to do. What to say. Who to talk to. You've only been back at school for a day, but you have a whole team. The people I sat with at dinner didn't even notice when I left."

"I've had a whole year, Lily, remember?"

"I know, but it's not like it was ever hard for you," I argue.

"What do you mean?"

"You had friends in high school," I say.

"So did you."

I want to tell him. I want to explain everything, but even after a year, there's still so much ground to cover between us. While he was playing sports and making friends and dating half the girls in our high school, I was planning a canned food drive and taking five AP classes. He didn't even really notice me at all, although he says he did, until last year when we started dating. And by then, he was already at school and he didn't see what it was like every day.

"I guess. I should just be social. I'm sorry. I told you it was stupid."

"It's fine. Go to a party or something. Join a club," he suggests.

"Maybe. I was invited to a party tonight, but I have to write an essay."

Derek sighs. "Don't do this, Lily. Don't be that girl."

"Be what girl?"

"Never mind. Just lighten up, okay? It's okay to have fun sometimes."

"I have fun," I tell him. "I have fun with you."

"I know, but I'm not going to be there every day. Like I said, this rugby schedule is intense, so I may not even be able to come up as much as I'd hoped. Don't sit around waiting for me."

It shouldn't hurt. I shouldn't be sad about it, because he's right. I spent most of high school "sitting around waiting" for Derek, but now, I don't have a clue how to start living my own life. I miss him, though. I miss something comfortable, something normal. Everyone else seems to slip into newness so easily.

"I won't. You are coming this weekend, though, right?" I ask.

"I am. Hey, listen, I gotta get going, though, okay? We're heading to a party. Jon says hi. And seriously, Lily…"

"Yeah?" I prod when he doesn't continue.

"Just… don't be weird, okay?"

"I'll try," I agree. After he says goodbye, I think about what he said. I'm in my pajama pants and a tank top, but Lyle said they were just having something small and it's only on the floor. It's not like I can't go for an hour or so and still make it back to do my homework. I mean, people balance things all the time.

I decide against going in my pajamas after all, but I do put my work away and get dressed. When I'm presentable, I head out into the hall. *You can do this. It's just a small group. You're not going to fail out of school if you stay up an hour later*, I tell myself. Of course, since I'm yet again not paying attention, I turn the corner by the elevator and walk right into someone.

"Oh, hey. It's Elinor."

"Lily. And I'm sorry about earlier." The momentary emptiness I saw in his eyes is gone now. He looks down, tugging at the hem of his shirt. It's an old shirt,

31

probably worn too often, and he looks young when he tugs at it. However, when he makes eye contact again, the wildness I sensed before has returned.

"No need. You were right. Marianne is a little flaky. I suppose I just like characters who don't have everything in place already." It's not directed at me, just a casual comment about a fictional character, but it reaches into the marrow of my doubt and gnaws at me.

"There's nothing wrong with a plan. With order."

"Okay, Lily. Let's try this again. I'm Jack... and you're Lily. You have read *Sense and Sensibility* several times, you apparently live on this floor, and you're a freshman. What else is there? Any deep, dark secrets just waiting to come out?" It's teasing, but I try to shake the question.

"How'd you know I was a freshman?" I ask.

"You look a little afraid someone's going to realize you're in the wrong place," he says.

"Am I?"

"I think that's your call."

"I'm going to a party," I tell him, although he didn't ask.

"Sounds grand."

"Do you... do you want to come?" Lyle didn't say I could bring anyone, but it feels like the polite thing to do.

"I can't. I've got plans, but I'll see you around, Miss Dashwood." He gives a half bow and leaves me standing there, confused. Do I really look lost to other people, too?

There are only five people in Lyle's room – him, Kristen, the condom hoarder whose name is Kendra, Don, and someone I haven't seen before. He introduces himself as Paul, but he doesn't seem to be interacting with anyone else.

"Paul's my roommate," Lyle says. "We've accepted we have nothing in common." Paul nods in response and goes back to listening to music.

Kristen is sitting between Lyle's legs and he has his arms wrapped around her. Her blond hair is falling into his cup of soda, but he's focused far more on flirting with her anyway. I settle next to Kendra. Don leans across her to hand me a cup of root beer.

"My boyfriend's at a party tonight," I tell Kendra.

"That's good." I'm not sure what I expected her to say or why she would care. I imagine Derek, thinking of all his stories, remembering the things he and Jon did in high school. It's a dramatically different world from sitting on someone's floor in a circle of five people, drinking soda, and awkwardly trying to make conversation.

"Lily, you up for a game?" Don asks. He tosses a controller in my direction. I'm terrible at video games, but Kristen and Lyle are occupied and helping Don take out zombies feels better than getting up and admitting this was a mistake.

Rebecca Ellison was pretty, it was true. However, she was unbelievably dumb. I don't mean she did poorly in some classes or struggled with a learning disability or that she had book smarts but no common sense or vice versa. She was honestly one of the dumbest people I had ever met. Still, dumb didn't matter, because she was pretty.

I'd heard it from Abby first. Derek had never been subtle about girls – not since the beginning of the year when he and Jon had started playing soccer and they became popular and I was just the nerdy little sister who still liked playing cards in a tent. Derek didn't change, though. Not really. Everyone else did and he fit right into their changing. He got his braces off and he played sports and suddenly everyone realized he was cute and *there was no way the quiet girl who spent her weekends reading and who knew the fifty states in alphabetical order and who was still afraid of getting her dresses dirty could compete with Rebecca Ellison.*

"Derek and Rebecca Ellison are a thing," Abby told me in history. "I guess they hooked up at Stacey Klein's party last weekend and it got a little crazy."

"I'm trying to learn about Ivan the Terrible," I said. "I don't care what Derek does." But we both knew better.

"She's not the first, you know," Abby continued. "I heard he's not a virgin already. Jaylinn told me that she heard from Tara that Derek hooked up with Heather Yost earlier in the fall."

I remembered hearing about it when it had happened. I'd been home, reading and eating cereal, and Jon and Derek came back from a party smelling like weed and beer. My parents had been out of town for the night for my father's job and Jon was in charge of me while they were gone, although it was me who ended up mopping up his vomit. Before he puked, though, I could hear him and Derek in the hallway, talking about Heather, and I didn't want to think about the things they were saying. It had only been a few months since we'd gone camping, but the boy I knew didn't talk like that.

"I know. But it's not my problem. What is my problem is the medieval nation-state of Russia, so unless Jaylinn or Tara has some interesting gossip about that, I need to focus."

It was a lie, of course, but what could I do? Aside from impaling myself on one of the great tsar's stakes and mourning the loss of something that was never going to happen, I mean. I almost made it through the day not letting it bother me – much – until I got to gym class. It was the only class I had with Rebecca and really the only reason I knew she existed. Earlier in the year, she'd "accidentally" bent over during volleyball when she forgot she wasn't wearing underwear. And then giggled when Wendy Nordstrom told her to "put away her vagina." It had been the biggest story that week, until someone else did something dumb. I don't really remember. It was easier to keep track of military coups than what girl did what with whom in my school.

When I saw her, I wanted to be mad. I wanted to be able to say she was ugly, that I wasn't jealous, that she was boring and that Derek would lose interest quickly, but she was standing on the track, which we were walking because our gym teacher had gotten bored with teaching us sports we couldn't play, and her hair was literally glowing. She had a damn halo, I swear, and I wanted to hate her. I wanted her beautiful golden locks to fall out of her head, but I couldn't really be angry at her. It wasn't her fault she was pretty. It wasn't her fault Derek liked her and she liked him. I couldn't blame her for wanting to be happy.

"Oh, my God. Lily!" She ran across the track towards me as if we'd ever spoken before. "You're Jon Drummond's sister, right?"

"Yup. Lily Drummond. Jon Drummond. Easy to make that connection," I said.

She didn't laugh; instead, she actually said the words, "ha ha ha." Followed by "you're so funny and cute."

"Okay." I wasn't trying to be cute. I was trying not to determine the likelihood of a time machine and the value of trade for someone like Rebecca in medieval Siberia.

"Can you believe they're making us walk this track?" she asked. "It's like a gazillion miles long, right?"

"A quarter."

"What?"

I sighed. "It's a quarter of a mile. That's why we walk it four times when we're timing a mile," I tried to explain. We'd been walking the track for more than a month – every single day. Every day, we had to time a mile. That was the entire assessment. We were even supposed to be keeping logs, so we could eventually do mathematic calculations that had yet to be revealed to us. "You know... the logs? We keep logs?"

"Huh? Oh, I don't know. I don't know anything about trees." I couldn't even form a reply before she said, "Anyway, I'm having a party this weekend. Can you tell your brother?"

"Sure."

"Great. Thanks," she said, before heading back to her friends who were still standing in a circle waiting for her. She sashayed. I'd seen the word in books, but I'd never experienced it. Thanks to Rebecca Ellison, I will always know what it is to sashay.

I make it through the week otherwise unscathed. All my work is done, I seem to be maybe becoming friends with Kristen, and Derek's on his way up to campus. I've been pacing for the better part of an hour.

"You need to relax," Kristen says. "What could go wrong?"

For people who don't need things in their places, it's easy to relax. If something goes awry, it can always be fixed later. For people like me, though, everything can always go wrong. When I can't control it, I panic. It's the only thing I know how to do.

"What if something's happened?" I ask for the third time. He was supposed to be here an hour ago.

"Nothing happened. He hit traffic, I bet."

"But why didn't he call?"

"Because he's an idiot. Now sit down and stop pacing. You're making me nervous."

There's a scuff on the toe of my shoes, so I do sit down. I scrub at it, but it won't come out; my attempts end up making it worse, so now the entire toe is dirty. "I look like hell," I tell Kristen.

"You look fine – just like you have for the last few hours when you've asked. How long have you been dating again?"

"Ten months."

"Ten months, and you think he's going to show up having not seen you in a week and realize he must have been crazy?" she asks.

"It's just... he's the only boyfriend I've ever had."

"So?"

How do I tell her about Rebecca Ellison, about Heather Yost, about Jill Pevarski, about Gina Frey, about all the girls Derek's dated? How do I explain that nothing ever seemed to happen, that one day he was with them and then one day he wasn't? How do I make her see that I've only wanted him and he fits into the puzzle and that I don't have a backup plan?

"Never mind. Can I borrow your shoes? The black ones you wore yesterday?"

Kristen shakes her head and jumps down off her bed. "Lily, none of it matters. If Derek doesn't want you, you're good enough without him."

Good enough is not good enough, I think. *No one wants good enough.* I don't say anything, though, but I take the shoes and change them. There's no sign of the scuff. Nothing is out of place, nothing out of order.

****

Derek's talking about traffic, but everything is fine now. He's here. The local diner was the only place I could think of to go for dinner that wasn't the cafeteria, but Derek seems perfectly okay with it as he douses his fries in ketchup.

"So how was the first week anyway?" he asks.

I stir my milkshake. I ordered it thinking I would have the appetite for it, but after one sip, I don't feel like eating or drinking. My nerves are frayed, which will pass, but a milkshake is dreadful right now. "It was all right. I missed you."

"I missed you, too. We have the whole weekend, though. Just us."

Kristen already made arrangements to stay with another girl on our floor, whose roommate went home to get a few things she'd forgotten, so Derek and I have some privacy. I was a virgin before Derek and I began dating, but over the past year, he's been my first kiss, my first boyfriend, and my first everything.

He leans across the table. "I don't know about you, but I could *definitely* skip the movie." We're supposed to see a movie with everyone, but being close to Derek, thinking about spending time together, messes with my head. I don't like to break plans.

"I promised, though," I argue.

"They won't care. Come on, Lily. We only get to see each other for a few days and then I won't be able to come up until next month."

"Next month?" He'd been vague when I'd asked, talking only about how much he was enjoying rugby practice and what my brother's been up to and asking about my classes. I should've known he was putting off telling me something.

"Yeah, but I don't want to focus on that," he says, stopping the discussion before it can begin. "So why don't we skip the movie? I'm sure your friends won't mind. You'll be able to spend plenty of time with them after this weekend and I know I've been thinking about nothing but being alone since you left."

We'd spent the day before we left for school locked in his room all afternoon, but I wanted to talk to him tonight. I wanted advice and I wanted to introduce him to people. I wanted to make him a part of what I'm trying to start here, but he's right and it's not worth arguing.

"Sure, I'll text them," I agree. I turn off my phone after I do, because I don't want to deal with the questions. There's no point in trying to explain; it's just a movie.

Derek goes back to talking, this time about a party he'd been to the night before. "Jon was a mess. You should've seen it," he says and takes a bite of his burger. I continue to stir my milkshake. When Derek finishes his fries, he grabs mine from my plate. I wasn't eating them anyway. "There were girls all over him, though, so he thought it was a success."

"What about you?" I ask.

"What do you mean?"

"Do girls hang all over you, too?"

He pours ketchup all over my fries. They're more splattered tomato than food now, but it doesn't stop him from eating them. I feel like I'm going to throw up.

"Well, yeah, of course, but I behave. Don't worry."

"I won't," I lie. "I trust you."

"You better," he says and he finishes the last few fries before throwing money on the table. "Let's go. I am dying to be alone with you. It's all I've thought about for days."

*Telling Derek how I felt didn't go how I'd expected.
I'd never really had a plan for it, assuming it would
never amount to much. Since I had realized it myself, he
was always seeing someone. Although Rebecca ended
up being over quickly, it established a pattern. He would
end up hooking up with someone at a party or
something, date them for a while, and it would end.
Sometimes it ended before he hooked up with someone
else, and other times it didn't. He earned something of a
reputation, but it didn't stop girls from trying and it
didn't change the boy I knew. Every so often we would
be sitting in my house and Jon would be doing
something or Derek would help my mom with the
groceries or I would just look up and I would notice that
the act faded for a moment. In those glimpses, short as*

they were, I saw the Derek I imagined and the one I loved. But that still didn't mean I had any intention of telling him.

I'd just turned 18 and Jon had brought Derek home for the weekend for my birthday party. Because it was me, my party was me, Abby, my parents, and the guys out at Olive Garden, but I had a hard time focusing because Derek was there and he kept looking at me. I would look up from my fettuccine Alfredo to find his rich brown eyes trained on me. At one point, I nearly choked on the forkful of pasta I'd been eating because he smiled and it was the kind of smile I remembered. He saw me and it might have been the first time in four years.

Later that night, after we'd had cake and everyone had gone to bed, I sat in my room rereading the card Derek had given me. It didn't say much and it was the kind of card you give your nephew when he turns three - it had a monkey on it and said "I'm going bananas wanting to wish you a happy birthday" – but he'd written, "I still remember that afternoon when we went camping." I didn't know what to make of it and I wanted to call Abby and ask her, but she'd had to go home early because she was going to her cousin's wedding and I was sitting up alone after midnight trying to make it make sense.

When he knocked, I didn't even think before inviting him in. I wasn't thinking about him being in my room or my parents finding us. I just wanted to understand what he was trying to tell me. During dinner, he had been telling my mom about Jodie, a girl he was dating at school, and I wondered if he even knew how much every word hurt me.

"Hey," he said, shutting the door behind him.

"Hi." I held up his card. "Thanks for your card. I was just... reading it. I mean, I remember that day, too. I just didn't think-"

I had always imagined my first kiss. In all my fantasies of it, it was with Derek, but I thought it would be romantic and I thought I'd be ready. When he came towards me, though, I froze. I didn't move as he lifted me out of my chair and kissed me, his tongue moving inside of my mouth, and it was nothing like I'd expected. He was demanding and I wasn't sure it was what I'd wanted or hoped for, but he smelled like he always did – a mix of soap and boy – and I wanted to stay close to him and I wanted whatever made him look at me over dinner to continue.

"What are you doing?" I asked when he stopped kissing me and smiled again.

"When did you get so damn sexy?" he asked me, his hands lifting my t-shirt and gripping my waist.

"Derek, I've never... I mean, I haven't even kissed anyone before. Well, I mean, I hadn't..."

I didn't have the words. My parents were sleeping in the next room and I knew what happened when girls let boys into their rooms and I could hear my mother warning me about screwing up my plans and I knew she'd tell me I was acting like a slut and I should have more self-respect, but I had spent four years dreaming about Derek and I didn't know how to say no.

"Shhh. I'll be gentle, Lily. Come here," he said and he led me to my bed.

It had been tough to watch him for years, knowing that he had girlfriends and thinking about what he did with them. I used to be jealous every time he would be at my house, talking about a date he went on. I heard the things he said, and I heard the stories at school. I knew they were probably true, but despite it, I couldn't help that I wanted him to do it with me, too. But when he was there and it was something that was actually happening, I didn't know what I wanted.

"No, wait," I told him.

He sat up, but he didn't let go of me and I was distracted by his hands. All of the thoughts and voices of everyone I knew were screaming inside my head. Abby telling me to go for it, that this was all I'd wanted for years. My mother lecturing me on what good girls do and don't do. My brother and the way I used to hear him and Derek talk about girls when they didn't know I could hear them. I didn't want to be like those girls, but I didn't want him to stop, either. I wanted the answer to be like school. I didn't want to guess what was right or okay.

"What about Jodie?" I asked. "Aren't you seeing Jodie?"

"How do you feel, Lily? What do you want? You've always wanted this, haven't you?"

"Yes, but if you knew... why now?"

He kissed me again and this time I didn't stop him when he lifted my shirt higher. "I don't know, but when I saw you at dinner, I realized what an idiot I'd been.

You've been right there in front of me for how long? And I just missed it. I want to make up for all that lost time. Don't you?"

I did and he said the right things and he whispered that he loved me and that he would protect me and that it was okay to feel like this and to want this and I gave Derek everything because I thought it was what I always wanted and he promised that I was different from all the other girls.

The glow-in-the-dark stars look pathetic in the darkness. There are only about twelve and they don't look like the night sky; instead they look like they got lost in the black and can't find their way back to light.

Derek's snoring, having fallen asleep quickly, but I can't stop thinking. My mind is doing that thing it does when I overanalyze and make problems where there aren't any and I want to turn it off. I want to be happy with my boyfriend's arm draped over my body. I want the closeness to feel like it should.

Maybe I read too many books. I guess I always thought being in love would feel comfortable. It's not that Derek doesn't try, but sometimes I'm so afraid. If he pauses too long when I ask him if something looks okay or if his upper lip twitches like it does sometimes when I do something wrong, I can't escape the doubt. Worry is like an endless ocean and my arms are just too tired to keep swimming.

I slip out from under his arm and head to the bathroom. I don't really have to go, but lying in the dark room isn't putting my mind at ease and so I pace the hall. The lights flicker, poor illumination because they're an afterthought; dorm halls aren't somewhere people spend their time. I consider going to find Kristen, or texting Abby even though I know she's in some foreign city and it will cost too much and she's probably doing amazing things. I even consider calling my parents to admit something is broken in me. But I can already hear the arguments. *I'm fine. Everything is fine.*

"Scottie dogs? What a fashion statement."

Jack's coming out of the elevator, carrying a guitar case. I almost start to cry knowing someone is seeing me like this.

"Sorry. I was just..." I look around. I wasn't *just* anything. I'm standing in the dim hallway by the elevator in the middle of the night wearing my pajamas.

"Yeah, I was just..., too," he says. "Want some coffee? I hear the lounge is lovely at this hour. There's all the Styrofoam a lady could desire."

"I-" I'm about to tell him I have a boyfriend, that I can't just drink coffee with him, but that's dumb. What's wrong with coffee? Derek's asleep, I'm restless, and it's just coffee. It certainly beats standing around by the elevator trying not to cry. "Sure. Coffee sounds good."

"Awesome. Let me just drop this off and grab some, okay?" He gestures to his guitar case and I follow him. He's just down the hall – in the guys' wing – and I make mental note of his room number. I don't know why I do, but it's etched on my brain before I realize what I'm doing. 401. Jack in 401.

"Did your roommate go home for the weekend?" I ask. He opens the door, tosses his case into a dark room, rummages loudly and knocks something over, and closes it again, coffee in hand.

"I don't have a roommate."

"Oh. I didn't know there were singles here."

He stops and looks at his door, then down at his shoes. "It's... a long story. Anyway, coffee?" When he looks up, there's a distinct change in his expression. It's pain wrapped in fear of acknowledging it; I know the look well.

In the lounge, he makes coffee, but the machine is old and the water is from the fountain in the hall, so the coffee just tastes like heat. There is no flavor or pleasure in drinking it, except it's warm and it's quiet in the lounge. Jack is picking the Styrofoam cup apart as he drains it. I don't know why it feels like normal. I thought I knew normal, but suddenly this feels like what it should have been all along.

"So you're not a freshman?" I ask.

"Junior."

"Your major?"

"Game Design. And you're English."

"How'd you know?"

He's finished turning the cup into pieces and he swaps the pile between his palms, looking at me the entire time. His eyes have danced through every human emotion in the few short interactions we've had. I didn't know anyone had the kind of depth I see in them.

"Lucky guess. Plus you've read *Sense and Sensibility* several times, which seems like an English major thing to do," he says.

"Yet you know the character names," I point out.

"Yeah, but I'm not..." He shakes his head. I don't know what the sentence was supposed to end with, but he's not continuing. "Besides, you came out of Joliet Hall, which is Humanities. I suppose you could just be taking a lit class, but it seemed a decent guess."

"Well, you're right. I'm predictable," I say.

"I don't doubt that, Elinor," he replies, but it's not judgmental. There's sadness in the way he says it. Regret. *Regret? Stop putting your own issues on him*, I tell myself. "So what brings you here?"

"To Bristol?"

Jack stands and throws out the Styrofoam. Each piece falls into the trash can like a heartbroken snowflake, slowly at first and then finally accepting its fate and taking the last few inches as inevitable. I watch them fall from his hands, his fingers outstretched and shaking. The ink on his arms is striking against the paleness of his skin.

"To sitting in a lounge with me in the middle of the night," he says. "You're predictable, as you said yourself." He turns back towards me. "So what's out of place?"

"Who said anything was?" I ask.

"I think I've misunderstood," he says. "I didn't mean to assume. I just thought there was something familiar in the way you were pacing."

"How so?"

He shrugs. "I've spent many nights pacing, too. And a lot more feeling like it was never going to make sense. I shouldn't have guessed that something was missing, just because it usually is for me."

My own Styrofoam cup, now empty, pays the price. How can he see so directly into the weakest parts of me? How does he know that the pieces don't fit? I picture my mother standing here, whispering in my ear that I'm slipping, that I'm pathetic, that I need to straighten out. I see my life and all my plans ahead of me and I feel them becoming faint outlines and I have to crush the cup to hold onto something solid.

"Thanks for the coffee," I tell him. "But I need to get back. I'm…"

I'm about to apologize, but he nods and walks away, leaving me alone. I stand up and throw what's left of my cup into the trash, where its mangled corpse hides the damage he did to his.

"I was thinking of trying out for the school play," I told my parents at dinner. Jon looked at me and rolled his eyes, but he didn't say anything.

"That sounds great, honey," my dad said, but my mom's face grew tight. I knew I had said something wrong, although I didn't know what was wrong with school plays.

"Is that okay, Mom?" I asked.

She didn't answer right away, her knife growing faster as she cut her chicken. I wanted her to nod, to say she'd be proud, but her lips were pinched and she finally sighed, dropping the silverware loudly against the plate. I felt the crashing in my skin, the sound of being wrong bleeding in my veins.

"Lily, you have a lot of responsibilities. I just can't understand why you would want to sacrifice your grades and what you've worked for. Have you even thought this through?" she asked.

"They said rehearsals are from 3-5 a few days a week. I can still go to NHS and Student Council meetings and I already asked Coach Hillary about alternating."

"And when are you going to do your homework? Between running, workouts, your clubs, and learning lines, you don't think your grades will slip?"

I looked at my brother, who was eating and not paying attention. He played sports, but he barely passed his classes. No one cared. He never needed to study. He was always out with his friends and my mother bragged about him endlessly, especially when he started dating Brianna Graves. She couldn't get enough of telling him how great Brianna was. Brianna, the valedictorian cheerleader who had no flaws. Brianna, who came over after school when my parents weren't around and locked herself in my brother's room with him, doing things I always found out about later when it filtered back to me through gossip. Things that led to her and Jon skipping school to go to a clinic out of town where *they could pay someone to make sure no one else knew that they weren't perfect.*

"I'm a junior. You won't let me work. It's only a few hours a week. I can ask for a small part," I argued.

"And what's the point then?" my mother snapped. "You're going to sacrifice for what? To get five minutes on stage? Do what you like, Lily, but I'm not going to sit there and pretend to be proud that you're an elf. If I thought you could handle a leading role, I might consider it, but you know what you'll do. It will all end up being too much and then you'll be here one night crying that you can't keep up with everything. I just don't want to hear it when you screw this up."

That was the end of the conversation, as far as she was concerned, although I did go to auditions. I practiced for two weeks after everyone was in bed, memorizing the monologue I'd found online. But on the day of auditions, I sat in the back of the auditorium. The girls were all so much more talented than I was, full of confidence and sure that they belonged on stage. They all knew they had something to say and that someone wanted to listen.

I was the last person to go. I waited until the end and all I could think about was how I wouldn't be able to get it right, how I'd forget the lines, how I would make a mistake and everyone would laugh. But when they called my name, I walked up on stage and pretended it didn't terrify me. The lights drilled their ghostly white through my skull and the kids directing were only fuzzy shapes, orbs of flickering color surrounded by faded darkness. My throat was dry, my tongue too big and stuck to the roof of my mouth. We weren't given anything but a stool, which I leaned on to stop the vertigo. But then I paused and breathed and I looked at the words in my shaking hand.

Inside the words, I could hide. I could become and the stage lights reminded me of what had sparked the desire in the first place. Becoming – not acting, not pretending, but <u>becoming</u>. That was what this was for me. And as I shed myself, a girl spoke... and everyone listened.

11.

Derek isn't listening. We've spent the entire weekend in my room, not even leaving to eat except to meet the delivery guy, but after two days, I still don't feel like he's hearing me at all.

"I'm saying I just wonder if it was a bad idea," I repeat. "I mean, yeah, this is a better school, but I don't know. Maybe I'd be happier with you and Jon. You could introduce me to people."

He leans back against the wall, knocking loose one of the pictures I put up. It was taken over the summer and we're both smiling in it. It was at a baseball game and although I'm not much of a fan, Derek had a great time and that night, he told me he saw his future and it was all me. I pick up the picture and try to smooth down the crease from where he bent it and pulled the tape from the wall.

"Lily, you wouldn't be happy. *I* wouldn't be happy," he says.

"Why? Don't you want to spend more time with me? All you've said since you got here is how much you missed being with me."

"Yeah, but that's physical. You know that. You know how much I love to hold you. But if we were together all the time, wouldn't you get bored?"

The photo's crease goes through my neck. I look like a monster.

"I don't think so. I don't get bored with you," I tell him.

"Because it's always been like this. Me away at school and you at home. Now you're away at school, too, so it just means when I come to visit we have privacy. But nothing else is different. This works, Lily."

"We were happy this summer, though. I saw you almost every day and we were happy."

"I guess, but you weren't being clingy. Don't start being clingy. Besides, at school, things are a certain way. I have my friends and you'd feel out of place. We

64

never really ran in the same circles, you know," he says.

"Are you ashamed of me?" I ask.

For the last ten months, I never visited him on campus once. It always made sense, though, because Jon felt like it would be uncomfortable for me to share the room with him and Derek and although he hasn't said much, I know he's still not sure how he feels about his best friend sleeping with his little sister. Now, though, I wonder if Derek is part of that, too.

He leans forward, pushing me backwards onto the bed, kissing me and holding me close to him. "Do I look ashamed, Lily?"

I don't have a chance to reply. He moves fast and I don't want to fight and he loves me. Obviously he loves me. So even though he doesn't answer my question directly, I let him keep kissing me and I believe what he says with his body because the words never come.

****

When Derek leaves, I don't know what to do with myself, so I go to the Club Fair. It's been happening all weekend, but my boyfriend took precedence over the Knitting Club. However, now that he's gone, Kristen and I are trying to be active or something. I look over at the frats and sororities for a moment; my mother would be delighted to be able to tell everyone about her darling sorority girl, but they're all just so... excited. I'm not excited. I'm cold and Derek was weird when he left, dodging questions about when he would call and he still never said whether he was ashamed of me and everyone here is happy and I'm not because there is something wrong with me. It hovers and swirls like an endless cyclone of doubt and chaos and I'm being swept away, which makes me angry. So angry that I turn around and join the Environmental Club before I can change my mind. *That will show them.* I don't know who them is and I don't think saving the planet is really a message that anyone should be upset about sending, but even my anger is pathetic.

I'm on an activity kick, though, so I just go down the line, signing up for things. Somewhere here is where I belong; somewhere is a place where I can feel less empty. I stop when I come to the drama troupe. I can still picture the auditions. I can even see the flickers of dust that darted across the burning lights. I feel the stage under my shoes, hard and hollow and echoing the fear with each step, but also unyielding and unforgiving enough to make me want to walk forward. I remember the silence while I spoke. People *listened*. For the only moment in my life, they truly listened, but then, it was over. When the cast list went up, I had gotten a part. I was to play Miss Prism, but it wasn't a lead. I'd said no on the form where it asked if I was interested in a leading role, but my mind seemed to tell me that if I was good enough, if I was perfect, they would cast me anyway. And Miss Prism was a good role. Four women were cast – and forty had auditioned. But my mother had been right and so I had declined. I consider all this in the moment as I pass the drama table. *Why bother if you can't be the best?* That's what my mother always told me.

"You should write for the paper," Kristen says.

"You think so?" I look over at the table. I enjoy writing. I like words, but I can't see myself being an aggressive reporter. Then again, how aggressive can you possibly have to be for the college paper?

"I think you'd be good at it. I mean, unless you're going to sign up for the Ping Pong Club?" She points to the table at the end, which is where we're headed. Since I've been mindlessly signing my name on things, it probably wouldn't be that much of a reach.

"Not that I have a thing against Ping Pong," I tell her, "but I'm kind of-"

"Dainty?" she asks.

"What the hell? I'm not dainty. What does that even mean?"

She laughs and grabs my pen, heading towards the newspaper table. "You just get a little OCD about random shit. You need to lighten up. Here. They need a music reporter. That's your calling, Lily. You are going to be Bristol's new punk princess."

"You look like a princess," my dad said.

My Prom dress was white and it was too long. There were bows and ribbons in places that didn't need bows and ribbons, but it was pretty and my mother had found it at some store in the city. And if it was good enough for people in the city, it had to be good enough for me.

"Do you think Derek will like it?" I asked Abby again. I'd been asking for weeks. He didn't want to go to Prom. He told me it was stupid to come home from school for something dumb like a high school dance, but I hadn't gone to Prom before and he had. Everyone had heard about his Prom.

"Yes. Calm down," she told me. "You look beautiful."

We were waiting for Derek and Jon. They'd both decided to come home, since Derek had to anyway for *me. I knew he had exams coming up and he hadn't been studying. We'd argued about it a few times, but I'd let it die because I didn't want to go to Prom alone. He didn't want to go at all.*

I grabbed Abby's arm and pulled her out into the hallway. "Do I look okay? I mean, do I compare to Gina?" Gina had won Prom Queen last year. The pictures were still in the albums by the couch in the living room – Derek and Gina, Jon and Brianna. I didn't know why my mom kept them. Jon and Brianna hadn't lasted past summer.

"Stop it, Lily. You look amazing. He'd be an idiot not to see that," Abby said.

She didn't know about the fight. She didn't know that I'd stayed up all night crying only two weeks earlier when Derek had said he thought I should go alone, that he had work to do, that it was a pointless tradition anyway and I wouldn't even like it.

He and I had been together almost six months. I wanted it to work. I was willing to sacrifice Prom for it to work, but he'd felt bad after making me cry. The next day, he had called back and he'd been genuinely contrite since. In my head, I envisioned him seeing me in the dress and feeling like an ass, begging for my forgiveness, but he was late and we had to take pictures and the limo was waiting and I was starting to wonder if I should have faked sick or something so everyone didn't have to wait.

"He's here," my mom called from the living room. Abby held my arm; she wanted to say something. There were moments when I thought she knew, when I felt like maybe I didn't need to try to find the words for the anxiety and fear I lived with, but she just shook her head.

When Derek walked in, he hugged my mom and then he looked at me, his eyes running over the length of my body. I was being inspected, but I hadn't been told in advance what the penalty was for failure.

"You look beautiful," he told me.

"So it was worth it?" I asked.

"I'm sure you'll make it worth it," he said, his hands moving quickly over every part of me before my parents noticed.

"Everyone in the living room for pictures," my mother yelled and we followed, obedient.

I stood with my boyfriend's arm around me while my dad called me his princess and my mother said she was proud. Finally I had done something that she could stick in a frame and preserve.

We took plenty of pictures, those cellulose storytellers we cling to when we want to believe the past was one way even though we know it wasn't. The shiny lies only reveal what's on the outside, what we can see, and the limitations of the senses tell a different truth. Derek smelled awful but the stench of weed that clung to his tux didn't get captured by the camera. In the end, the pictures were perfect and they could be placed next to the ones from Jon's Prom, all part of the façade. It didn't matter that the night was anything but, because it's only about what we allow ourselves to remember.

13.

Joining the paper has been good, because it keeps me busy. When I'm not working on schoolwork or attending my sporadic Environmental Club meetings with Lyle, I'm in the newspaper office. I don't know anything about music, but Kristen wasn't kidding. They wanted a music reporter and that's what I do. I open bins of CDs and take them back to my room and listen to them and try to write reviews, but it all sounds the same to me.

"Hey, you, new girl." My editor comes into the office as if we were already in the middle of a conversation. I save the inane review I'm writing, empty praise about some band who plays "Shoegaze," whatever that means, and turn around.

"Lily," I remind her, but she knows.

"Yeah, whatever. Listen, I need you to cover some crappy concert."

"Um, I don't know," I say. I've been to one concert ever, and it was a Christian folksinger who played at my church. "I really don't belong in music," I tell her, but I've told her and everyone else and despite the fact that the twelve people who read our paper know this as well, I'm still reviewing genres of music I didn't know existed. I wish I could just interview a math professor or something.

"It's fine. They're playing tonight," she tells me. "The band from campus that I need you to do the story on is the first opener, so you don't need to stay. Just take some pictures and get a quote from one of the band members and you're free to go."

"Do you know who they are?"

She rolls her eyes. "No. Some generic college band that will break up by next semester. But make them look good. Then they'll pass out copies of the paper."

"Great," I sigh and I get the address of the club.

I go back to the dorm and change into something I figure is rock clubby, which means jeans and a black shirt, since I actually have no concept of what people wear to concerts.

The "club" is actually an unfinished wood platform in the middle of a linoleum floor, some folding chairs, and a bar that could be outmatched by the one in my uncle's rec room. There are a decent amount of people here, though, which I guess must mean one of the bands is pretty good. Then again, maybe people just go to clubs regardless of what's happening.

"Five dollars," the guy at the door mumbles and holds out his hand. I show him my college ID, because my editor said she'd call ahead and get me on the list. The door guy looks at my ID and back at me. "Five dollars," he repeats.

"I'm supposed to be on some list," I explain.

"Does it look like I have a list?" It does not, as there is nothing but him and a stool out here.

"No, but-"

"It's five dollars. Are you coming or going? There are people waiting."

I look behind me, but there isn't anyone there. Grumbling, I take out money and pay to get in. "I need to interview the band," I tell the guy. He points vaguely towards the right of the stage.

I head in that direction, where a metal chair is resting in front of a black felt curtain. No one is anywhere around the curtain, so I peek through the felt.

The life of a rock star is not very impressive. I guess I always imagined musicians went backstage to giant suites filled with food and women and parties. Instead, it seems like the curtain leads to a small area by a loading dock, where the equipment is being unloaded out of a minivan by the band members themselves. The illusion is shattered for me forever.

"Hey, it's Elinor." Jack's standing behind a few of the guys and he drops his case, approaching.

"Are you in the band?" It's probably a stupid question, but I'm caught off guard seeing him again. I seem to run into him a lot.

"I am. What are you doing here? Doesn't really seem like your scene."

"Yeah? What is my scene?" I ask. I don't know why I feel like I need to prove something to him, but I want to be more than the lost girl who needs a plan for everything.

"I don't have a clue. I just didn't expect to see you here."

"Maybe I'm full of surprises."

"Maybe you are. So, do you want to come backstage?"

"Would that make me an unofficial groupie or something?" *Are you flirting? You cannot seriously be flirting.* My admonition is unjustified, since I wouldn't call it flirting exactly, but I do get a little giddy when he steps closer. "Are the stories all true about musicians?"

"What stories are those?" he asks.

"You know – wild nights, lots of women, tragic pasts."

He laughs bitterly. "You have no idea."

"So tell me."

"Lily, I'm not a good guy," he says. "I'm really not a good guy and I am most definitely not a guy who belongs with a girl like you. I should have made that clear before."

"Well, I have a boyfriend. I'm only here for the paper," I say, regretting the words as soon as I say them. I sound like a child; I wouldn't even be at a concert if it wasn't for my school club.

"Ah, okay. Sure, let me grab Neil, the singer. It's really his band," Jack tells me and he heads back towards the loading dock. He talks to another guy dressed all in black before heading outside and disappearing. For some reason, I can only say the wrong thing with this guy.

Neil tells me all about the band and his inspiration and I write it down verbatim, but I'm barely listening. I can't stop thinking about Jack's eyes and how much he makes me doubt myself. All of the things I've ever wanted seem stupid and meaningless when he talks to me, like paper dolls, translucent and insubstantial. My life is like a window dressing for a real person. But the fear that is ever present doesn't fade. I know what happens when you make mistakes. I know the price of not being perfect.

Her name was Lucy and she was beautiful. It had taken a lot of pleading, but when my father brought her home as a surprise, I couldn't believe it. She was mine, too. Jon said he had no interest in a dog, but I didn't care. I brought her right to my room and cuddled her and scratched her ears. She jumped on my bed immediately, undeterred by my mother's loud footsteps as she followed us.

"Lily, take that animal off your bed. I just made it," she yelled at me.

"Mom, she's fine. Look how pretty she is," I argued. My dad was standing behind my mom in the doorway. I'd been asking for weeks and I'd heard them whispering at night – my father saying it would be good for me, that I needed someone other than Abby and following after

Jon and Derek like I was lost. Abby's parents were always dragging her places and at eleven, I had no other friends. My mom just kept complaining about the mess, but obviously my dad had won.

"Let it go," my father interjected. "Lily's good. She'll take care of Lucy and she'll make sure everything's done right. Won't you, Lily?"

"I will, I promise," I agreed.

That night, I sat at the table while Lucy chewed on an old stuffed animal I gave her and my parents talked me through an elaborate daily schedule that involved walks and feeding Lucy and playing and cleaning up her poop. I didn't care; it all sounded wonderful.

"Don't forget that this means you're going to have to be responsible," my mother said. "It means you are going to have to figure out how to do these things and still go to dance class and still do your homework and still play softball. You can't start quitting everything just because you have a dog. People are counting on you."

"I know. I told you. I'll be perfect."

I was at first, too. It was late spring and everything was winding down, so I could balance all my responsibilities. And the summer was even better. I woke up to walk Lucy and then we went to the park and played and I made sure she was bathed and fed and my mom didn't even have to look at her; she didn't want to and whenever Lucy would try to show her affection, my mom told me to take her outside, but it didn't matter. I loved her and my dad was right; I was good and I was responsible and I wouldn't screw it up.

It was all because of math class. I'd gotten a B on my test and my mother was going to have a fit. I stayed after class to talk to my teacher, but he took too long coming back from the teachers' lounge and my bus left without me. School was almost two miles from home, but I knew what would happen. I knew I had to try and I ran. I ran harder than I had the lungs for and I ran because I had to get home. I had to make it and I had to take Lucy for her walk and make sure my mom never knew. The B alone was going to get me in trouble, but if I screwed up the schedule...

My knees hurt when I got home. Lucy was in her cage in the basement, where she slept while no one was home, but she had peed all over everything. I was nearly an hour late and she couldn't wait. Her gorgeous brown eyes were so ashamed, but it was my fault. If I had gotten an A like I was supposed to, I wouldn't have missed the bus and Lucy wouldn't have had to pee all over herself.

"It's okay, Lucy. It's okay. You wanna take a bath? Let's go for a walk and then bath, okay?" I asked. I knew I had to make the walk quick, because I had to get back, clean her off, and change the papers in her cage. I had to make it perfect.

I took Lucy for her walk, got her bathed, and I was changing her cage when my mom came home. Early for once. She'd had a headache and when she saw me carrying the papers, I was scared of what came next.

"What are you doing?" she asked.

"I'm just changing Lucy's cage."

"Did she have an accident?"

"Sort of. Mom, before you get mad at her, it was my fault. I missed the bus and I ran home, but she had peed and I'm almost done. I'm sorry. Please don't get mad at her," I begged.

Her face never changed expression. "Why did you miss the bus?"

"I was staying for help for math. We had a test and I missed a few questions."

"How many questions?" she asked.

I didn't want to tell her. Lucy was happily rolling around outside past the screen door and I wanted to play with her. I wanted to tell her everything was all right, but I knew it wasn't. I wanted to tell Lucy and I needed to believe it myself. "Just a few. I misunderstood something," I tried to explain.

"What was the grade?" I paused and she caught my hesitation. "Lily, if you cannot handle the responsibility of a pet and still maintain your grades, I think it's clear you are not old enough to have a dog."

"Mom, please. I got an 84, but it's only one test and my grade is still an A and my teacher is going to work with me and I promise I won't let it happen again."

She pushed past me, leaving me standing in the kitchen, her heels clacking heavily on the hardwood floors. "When you father gets home, I'm having him bring your dog back to the pound. Say your goodbyes if you must. Maybe in the future, you will take your responsibilities more seriously."

"Mom, no. Please," I begged, but she went upstairs and slammed her door. I shoved the pee-soaked papers in the trash and went outside, burying my face against

Lucy. She was sweet and perfect and I had screwed up and I couldn't handle it. I wasn't even twelve yet but I hated myself and I wanted to start again. I wanted to be a different person.

I tried to reason with my father that night, but he talked to my mom and he came outside after he did, where Lucy and I were playing in the last light before nightfall.

"I'm really sorry, honey," he said. I knew he was and I knew he was disappointed in me, too. But it didn't matter. I rode in the car with him and Lucy and I cried the whole time. I cried when he handed her off to the guy at the shelter and it broke me into pieces as she barked and looked at me while they closed the door.

I never saw her again. I tell myself sometimes that she was adopted by someone who was better than me, someone who could get it all right. I have to imagine her running and playing in a big yard. Her eyes haunt me and every time I see a dog who looks a little like her, I imagine it's her. The only alternative is to admit that there was just as much of a chance that they put her down if no one else came to take her, and I just can't live with making that big of a mistake.

I don't know how it's October. It seems like I just started school, but the days have become long blurs of studying, reading, writing, doing stuff for the paper, and actually making some friends. I have a few, which is odd. I don't normally have friends as in plural, so it's been a new experience being around more than one person at a time. Sure, it's mostly Kristen and Lyle, who've kind of become one entity quickly, but it still feels like something new.

Derek has been busy and we barely talk, but it's Columbus Day Weekend and we're all headed home and I can't wait to see him. I'm still not sure about being at different schools and I'm going to mention it again this weekend, when we've both had time to think about the idea.

Of course, they're late; they're always late. It doesn't matter, though. This weekend will be great. A chance to be home, to put everything back in order, to figure out how the past fits into the future. It's been like I'm living in two worlds, a fictional girl living a fictional life while the real girl is on pause. I need to go home again, to find the ground, to synthesize these two people fighting for space in my brain. I need to stop feeling like I'm so close to making a mistake.

"Are you coming back late Monday?" Kristen asks. "Or should I wait so we can all have dinner?"

"I think it depends on the guys, but I want to say Derek has practice, so probably. I'll text you."

She nods, but there are things she isn't saying. I know she worries, because I still have nights where I wake up and I can't breathe, so sure I'm going to mess up, but I try to hide them. Still, when you share a small space with a person, you're privy to the secrets they keep even from themselves.

"It'll be good. I feel like I need to go home, to remember who I am," I try to explain.

"Maybe that's the problem, Lily," she says. "Maybe you need-" She stops and closes the book she's reading, then thinks better of it and shakes her head. "Never mind. Have fun."

"I think they're here," I say, even though they didn't text and Kristen knows it. But the room, small already, feels claustrophobic. Her unfinished *comment* feels claustrophobic, because I know what she thinks of Derek. She tries not to say anything, but she gives me the same look every time I stay up most of the night waiting for him to call, only for morning to come without a word.

Outside, people are relaxing on the lawn while they wait for rides or just because it's mid-October and summer refuses to leave. Autumn is creeping into the landscape through the coloring of the trees, but even that seems like it's in slow motion. The seasons, although dictated by dates, function on their set of rules. I'm in a tank top and sandals when a few years ago, it had already threatened to snow by now.

I catch Jack sitting by the massive oak in the middle of the quad, listening to music and writing. I think of saying hello, of asking what he's up to this weekend, even though we haven't run into each other since the concert. He's only down the hall and I admit

I've looked for him, but he's never anywhere I go. For a couple weeks, he was everywhere, but since that awkward conversation in the club, our paths haven't crossed. It's probably for the best anyway.

Just leave him alone, I tell myself. *What's the point? Where is he going to fit into your life?* And although I know it's true, and I know there isn't a space carved out for someone like Jack – that I've never even known anyone like Jack, despite barely knowing him now, I can't help but be irritated. Just because there isn't a place doesn't mean there can't be. Isn't everything supposed to be fluid? Shouldn't life make room for something different?

They're stupid thoughts and stupid questions, and despite their ache in my mind, I sit down and wait for Jon and Derek. The familiar is always right; the familiar makes sense; the familiar keeps you safe.

****

"I see you found the cafeteria just fine." My mom's first words when I walk in the door, having not seen them in six weeks. "She's putting on weight, isn't she, Derek?"

He laughs and squeezes my arm. "You know what they say, Mrs. Drummond. Freshman 15 and all that."

I haven't gained fifteen pounds. I haven't gained even five pounds, but they laugh as if it's funny, as if making me a joke is how they prefer to spend their weekends. I feel Derek's fingers on my flesh, but for the first time, I don't want him touching me. I feel wrong when he does.

"What about you?" my mom asks him. "Anything new at school?"

"Just settling in. I'm playing rugby this year."

"Oh, that's great. Isn't that great, Lily? You should try that. Joining a club would be good for you."

"I'm in clubs," I remind her. I've told her several times, but she only asks what my grades are and how Derek is when she calls. "And the paper."

And like I didn't speak, she turns back to Derek and asks about his classes. I want to scream. They treat me like I'm naïve, childish, stupid. A fool. I want to tell them they're both wrong, but since I stand silently taking it like a fool, maybe they're not the ones who are.

"Will you be staying for supper?" She's on a roll tonight. Maybe my dad and I should go get hot dogs and let my mom and perfect Derek discuss his rugby stardom over dinner.

Why are you angry at him? It's not his fault, that little voice tells me, but I disagree. Jon and Derek can do no wrong, but no matter how hard I try, no matter what I give, it's just never enough for her, and that does make me angry at him. Maybe it's not his fault, but he's never once defended me in the time I've known him and he's seen it for years. I don't know why this is all irritating me so much right now, but it is and it does and there's not much else to be done, is there?

"I can't," he says. "I need to head home. I'm beat."

"You just got here," I reply.

"I know, but it's late and I'm worn out. I'll come by tomorrow and we can do something, okay?" He leans over and kisses the top of my head, something that has always been his sign of affection for me but it just makes me feel young again.

"Can you call me later?" I ask.

"Don't beg," he answers. "It looks pathetic. I'll see you tomorrow."

Waking up the day after my birthday was weird. I wasn't a virgin anymore and I'd had this night that I had thought about for years, but in the morning, something about it felt wrong. I told myself it was because Derek had gone back to Jon's room immediately after, telling me he didn't want anyone to find us together, but I wasn't sure, as the sun came up, that there wasn't more. I hadn't said no. I hadn't wanted to say no – not really. But it had been sudden and I hadn't thought it would happen and then it did and I couldn't take it back and there was no big ceremony to address the fact that a part of who I was no longer existed.

Abby had already had sex, but it had happened with Tony Ellroy, a guy she'd been seeing and they had planned it and spent the weekend at a hotel his cousin booked for them. She'd told me Tony had been shy and he'd brought flowers and grape juice because they weren't old enough for wine, and that both before and after the actual deed, he had told her she was more beautiful than sunsets. It sounded cheesy at the time, but in my room, alone, feeling somehow less than I'd been the day before, I wanted to be more beautiful than anything. Aside from Derek calling me sexy and reminding me that I'd pined for him for years, he didn't say much. And the little he'd said certainly wasn't about sunsets.

I waited for a while, thinking maybe he would sneak back in, find a stolen moment in the chaos of morning, but no one came. I heard everyone moving and I could smell breakfast, but my door never opened. Eventually, I got up and put on jeans and a sweater, even though it wasn't that cold despite being November, and I tried not to cry.

No one prepares a girl for the moment when she allows someone access to herself. When you're still a virgin, there's this aura around you. You're untouched and unsullied. It's almost like being superhuman because everyone else has quiet moments in dark places when they become base animals but not you. You are intact. As a girl you're told to treasure this part of yourself. It defines you. You are good while you're a virgin. Pure and perfect. But when it's gone, it's just gone like that. Maybe you got lucky - no pun intended - and it was something magical and fulfilling but most likely it wasn't. Most likely it was just like it was for me. Awkward and weird and painful and disappointing and, worst of all, intrusive. While he washes you off of himself, just a place he visited, he's been inside of you. He will forever have been there and there is no way to remove him. And the first time? Even if he physically didn't break through that barrier, so to speak, he will always own that part of you. That piece that was yours and was perfect and unbroken is now his. Forever. And you can't ever forget that or make it not true. While Derek was with me, I enjoyed it on a sensory level, but I felt like I'd been drained of the only thing that made me worthwhile.

"Lily, are you coming down for breakfast?" My dad was in my doorway and I wondered if he could tell. I wondered if he looked at me and saw the shame, if he sensed that I was missing a piece. I felt like I had let him *down, that the night before, on my birthday, I had sat at dinner and I was his daughter and I was whole. Now I wasn't. Whether Derek loved me or not was not even discussed. Someday, if I moved on or if he did, he would always be the person who owned something of mine.*

I shook my head. "I am. Sorry. I was just thinking."

"It's your birthday. Don't look so sad, honey."

I wanted to run to him, but I dug my feet into the carpet. The polyester fibers scratched at my toes, and I pushed down on them until it hurt too badly to ask my dad to hug me.

"I'm okay, Dad. I'll be down in a minute."

After he left, I went into the hall and I looked towards Jon's room. The door was open and the shades were up. I could hear Derek and Jon's voices from the kitchen, chatting about school, and I stood in the upstairs hallway, crying, because it was my fault and I had wanted it and why couldn't I be happy? Why couldn't I be normal?

By the time I made it downstairs, the puffiness was gone around my eyes and I smiled when I saw him at the kitchen table. He got up and made a big gesture of pulling my chair out for me.

"Can I tell them?" he asked loudly as he pushed me into the table.

"Tell us what?" Jon asked.

"Last night, Lily and I talked and... well, Mrs. Drummond, you wouldn't mind her having a college boyfriend, would you?"

My mom glowed at the idea.

I had pacified her. I had proven I could be good enough and Derek and I could succeed where Jon and Brianna had failed and she would have everything she wanted. It didn't matter to her that Derek hadn't asked me a thing, including whether I was ready. It didn't matter to anyone that my body ached because I'd done things I suddenly wanted to wash off, that I hadn't planned on doing yet. I told myself that what I had given up for that smile was worth the price. Anything was worth the cost to feel like maybe I hadn't failed for once. I believed that, because I had to believe it.

There are only two reasons people in town come here, to the hill that looks over the river, and neither has to do with the way that the sun glares off the ruins of the factories that built, and eventually ruined, our town. One reason is to have sex, and Derek and I know the area well. We've spent many evenings, and some afternoons, up here, when my parents were at home or Jon was or he just wanted to do something different. It's not romantic, but it's secluded because it used to belong to the factories and now only the ghosts of those lives remain.

The other reason people come up here seems inexplicably linked to that history. It's oddly both a place where couples go to be together – and also to grow apart. Throughout high school, almost everyone broke up with someone here, like there is pressure in the air that you need permanence to exist in such a place and, without it, you realize there is little worth clinging to in your relationship.

"I've been thinking a lot about what you said," Derek starts, "about transferring."

I turn in the backseat of his car to face him. The weather is still insisting on summer regardless of the calendar and I'm sticky and warm. Derek turned the car off when we arrived and now, in a barely acceptable state of undress, I'm trying to find my underwear and he's looking out the window at the river.

"Good, I wanted to talk about that," I say. I find my panties somehow between two soda bottles and an old CD under the passenger seat. It was over before it even started, like requisite physical interaction without meaning. "I mean, I like Bristol. I guess I would love it eventually, but it's hard to be in two places at once. I feel stuck between home and school." He doesn't say in anything in response, but as soon as I say the words, "I think I'd be better off somewhere familiar, with you and Jon," he says the words I've dreaded since he acknowledged me for the first time.

"That's why I think we should probably take a break," he says.

"What do you mean?"

"It's just..." He pauses and cracks the window open more, but the suffocating air isn't because of the heat. I *need* to fix this. I can't screw this up. This is the only thing I've been able to keep intact, besides my schoolwork, and I can't just take tests and write papers for the rest of my life. "Look, Lily, I really enjoy spending time with you, but I like my freedom, too. Some of the rugby guys have been talking about renting a house and I feel like I'm trapped in this relationship with you, like I have to pass everything by you first," he says.

"I've never asked you for anything," I argue.

"Not exactly, but you need me and it's a little annoying."

"Oh."

I don't know what to say, because I should have seen this coming, I suppose. Instead of saying anything, though, I stare out my own window. The closest factory's windows have all been shattered and plants hopelessly try to grow through the damage. It's more depressing than if there was nothing there but ruin. Watching the life try to continue after everyone else has moved on just makes me think it's all futile. When we outlive our purpose, we should disappear. No one needs a reminder that they've failed.

"It's not a break up. Not really. We can still see each other when you want and I'll come up the weekend after your birthday so we can do something. I still care about you," he says, but the words feel rehearsed.

"The weekend after my birthday?"

"I have a match the weekend of and we're going to stay in a hotel for that weekend, so I'd rather spend the whole weekend with you the week after. Maybe we can go somewhere romantic," he says and methodically rests a hand on my knee. It's still uncovered, because I haven't found my pants yet. Why does it always seem like the moments when you're most vulnerable are the ones when you are missing something as obvious as pants?

"You just had sex with me," I whisper, but even at this volume, the comment feels too loud.

"Oh, Jesus, Lily. Really? Don't act like you're somehow pure and innocent. So we had sex. It was good. But we were never getting married. You can have sex with someone and still need a break."

"No, Derek, I can't. I can't do that, because I've never done that. I've never been with anyone else," I remind him.

"I don't have time for this shit," he says, sighing. "Things are crazy right now. I haven't seen you in a while and I have exams coming up and I can't spend all my energy on whatever issues you're making up in your head." He stops speaking, and it's painful. There's something he isn't saying, and I don't know if I want to hear it.

"What happened?" I ask, preparing myself for the worst.

"Nothing happened. Why is it always about you? I just have papers and exams coming up and things have gotten away from me. I'm so worried I'm gonna fail all my classes. I've been screwing around so much with sports and-"

"You're failing school?" It comes out judgmental, which I don't mean to happen, but it kind of annoys me. Derek's always been a mediocre student. He only passed his first year of college with my help, and now he's letting school slip and he's making that my problem. He's leaving me with nothing because he can't do it himself.

"I'm starting to wonder what I ever saw in you," he snaps. "For someone who has no clue and who needs me to pick up all her pieces, you certainly act like a bitch."

"Yeah, I wonder, too," I say. We have nothing in common. What kind of person chooses rugby over school? It's not even a real sport.

He reaches behind me and finds my pants tossed by the rear car window. I don't say a word and finagle myself into them and then go sit in the passenger seat. I just want to go home.

When Derek gets into the driver side, he pauses and looks at me and I want to remember. I want to see the boy I thought I loved, but in his eyes, there's nothing but this guy. I wonder if he was ever anything but this guy and I feel sick. He leans down to kiss me and I turn my head, trying not cry.

"Whatever, Lily. What the hell do you know, anyway?"

"Nothing. I think it's really, really clear that I know absolutely nothing," I say and we drive back to my house in silence. Everything that I left behind is floating off into the past like uncontrollable wisps of memory and I'm reaching out with nothing to hold onto. I guess this is the whole point of college and growing up and life in general, but I hate it. I hate that everyone always has the answers when you don't need them, but once you reach a point where you're surrounded by nothing but questions, you're standing alone in the middle of people who don't have a clue.

When Derek returned to school after my birthday, we didn't talk about Jodie. She was a fleeting idea at dinner and then she was gone. I didn't know if they had fought, if she'd already known about me, or if he made up another reason, but when I asked if we were dating, he said yes and I didn't want to dig deeper. So when her name came up in the spring, it felt ominous.

"Jodie and I were up all night trying to figure this out," he said. "I am never going to pass this class."

It was American History I – Revolution to Civil War, and I didn't understand what was so hard about it for him. We all had to take almost two years of the same content in high school. I wasn't even sure how he had gotten into college if he'd been this bad of a student. But when he said her name, I forgot all about Crispus

Attucks. With apologies that his death was secondary to Derek and Jodie, I took a deep breath and asked the question I had been afraid to ask for nearly six months.

"You and Jodie still hang out?"

"Yeah. Don't worry about it, Lily. I'm with you. She knows that and it's fine."

"You were up all night? At the library?" I asked.

"You aren't serious right now, are you? I'm going to fail and you're worried about there being a girl in my room? The whole world isn't like high school, you know. Don't be that girl."

So I wasn't that girl. I helped him learn about the Boston Massacre and he talked and I listened and I was good. I did the things he wanted from me, and that made me happy because I had always wanted Derek and love was about sacrifice and it was about trust and it was all the things I'd been told. But when I told Abby about the conversation and my fears and doubts over lunch the following week, it scared me when she voiced things I didn't know how to put words to by myself.

"You think he's cheating?" she asked.

"I don't know. I mean, he's right, I guess. It's just so high school of me to ask. So there was a girl. And so they dated before-"

"You mean they used to fuck. Don't play innocent. He fucks girls and he throws them away and you refuse to see anything but some guy you liked when you were fourteen. He's an asshole and he probably is fucking her. But he likes the idea of owning you, so he keeps you distant from it," she said.

"But he loves me. He wouldn't do that. He loves me. And he's right. I'm his girlfriend. I need to act like it and stop worrying," I argued.

"Is that what you're majoring in? Girlfriendship? I didn't know that was a thing."

"It's not like you're single. You're never single," I reminded her.

"So? I like the guys I date, but they're not who I am, Lily. When are you going to be Lily, and not Mrs. Drummond's daughter or Jon's sister or Derek's girlfriend or my friend? Who is Lily? Do you even know?"

I'd been picking at my lunch, but the conversation was too big for the cafeteria and it was too bright and too loud and I needed to talk about something normal. I needed life to be as easy to make sense of as things in packets and books and on the classroom walls. I felt like I was preparing for this obscene pop quiz and I had nightmares of showing up with only a giant green marker and I couldn't fill in the bubbles – not the right way – and I was going to fail. This quiz was my life and I was failing and that's too much to think about when someone is sitting next to you making a bong out of a Hawaiian Punch can and your tuna salad sandwich is soggy and the plastic circle seat of the table under your ass feels like it's going to spin off into space any minute.

"I have to go," I said and I nearly fell from the seat, my balance off kilter.

Abby said something, and it sounded meaningful, but the cafeteria was so loud. I couldn't make sense of anything except that she was right and I didn't have an answer for why I didn't do a thing about it. Nothing scared me more than not knowing the answer.

The rest of the weekend is unbearable. My mother glares at me as if she knows, but I didn't mention anything about Derek. Let her think she'll live her golden dream of us populating the world with perfect babies. I don't have the stomach or mind for telling her otherwise. But she glares and my dad tries to smooth it over, but he's lost so much of himself, too, in the last few years and the whole weekend is this incredibly odd distant reality. In a few weeks essentially, I can't make sense of anything. School felt alien but expectedly so, but home was supposed to remain the same. Consistent. Normal. And now I'm in this spiral where I can't remember when I am.

My mother angrily passes me a bowl of salad during lunch before we all head back to school and I almost feel like I should be asking about the school play again, because all of my memories and flaws are flooding the now with their insistent pleas that I find myself. I didn't even know I was lost until suddenly I was.

"I'm not hungry," I say and I pass the salad on to my father and Jon talks about some class he's taking that he probably doesn't even attend and I hate him. I hate my brother for the first time in almost nineteen years.

"Is there a girl in the picture?" my mom asks him.

"I'm keeping my options open," he replies. *You're keeping their legs open*, I want to retort, but it makes me feel bad about myself. It feels judgmental and petty, like it's their fault and I certainly don't want to fill my mom's head with this idea that any girl Jon brings home might be a slut. Because even if she is, it's not like she's being a slut all by her damn self, that's for sure.

By the time Derek shows up, I'm not prepared for the charade. He kisses me while I'm sitting at the table, brushing his lips over the top of my head and resting his hands on my shoulders. While he chats with my mom, the touch radiates in my blood. All of the intimacy, all of the memories are mocking shards of mistakes inside my body. He's been inside my body so many times and it doesn't matter. It was supposed to be special and I was supposed to be special, but special's a lie we tell girls to make them feel better about having to be broken just to grow up.

"Are you guys ready to head back?" he asks.

"We're still eating," I point out, although I haven't touched my food.

"I have practice," he says.

"Well, maybe the world doesn't revolve around you."

"Lily," my mom says, before turning to Derek to apologize. "She's been moody all weekend. I'm sure it's her hormones from all that weight she's gained."

"Don't worry about it, Mrs. Drummond. I'm used to it. Besides, girls don't care about sports, so I'm sure she doesn't understand." I ran track for four years, but I've given up on explaining to Derek that running is a sport. I don't bring it up now, either.

"Fine. Let's go," I say, getting up and grabbing my bag. "Wouldn't want you to be late."

Jon, oblivious, gets into the backseat as he's done for the last year when it was the three of us and I'm left debating between sitting next to him and letting Derek act like our driver or sitting next to Derek and pretending it doesn't hurt to see how easy it all is for him. It's still a toss-up when he wraps his arms around my waist and kisses my ear.

"I told you it was only a break. I just need to get things in order. Don't go forgetting all about me. I still care and I still want to see you," he says. "I'm going to make big plans for the weekend after your birthday. That's less than a month away. You'll see – it will be better this way."

"It will be better to put everything on hold while you decide if I'm good enough?" I ask, turning to face him.

"College is hard. I'm doing this for you," he says.

"No." I push him away, angry at the condescension in his voice. He might be older, but it's been a year. One. Fucking. Year. It's not like he's the world's leading expert on college life transitions.

"Okay, but you'll see. I'll be up in a month and I promise you'll be happier with this arrangement."

"Whatever," I say. I choose the passenger seat, mostly because Derek is on the other side of me and it's easier to walk away in that direction. Maybe I'm being childish, but I don't care. I can go back to school and work on my paper about Elinor and none of this is important. He's just a guy. It doesn't matter that he was always the only one. It doesn't matter that everything I've ever told myself is one giant, glaring lie.

****

Your analysis is shallow. It feels like you only understand emotion or humanity on a superficial level. Maybe try something that challenges your foundations, rather than grasping at them.

"She's gotta be kidding," I repeat to Kristen. She's been listening to me for the better part of an hour. "I'm not shallow. *She's* shallow. God, half the kids in the class didn't even read the book and I could recite the stupid thing."

"I don't know. I mean, I don't have any lit classes, but it could be good for you. She's right. Try something new. You do have a tendency to expect the future to look exactly like the past."

111

"You've known me for a month."

"Technically almost two, but I live with you, Lily. You don't like to be challenged, but maybe your professor is right. It's only a paper, so what's the worst that happens if you try something a little out there and it's a disaster?"

"Um, I fail," I say.

"One paper?"

"Okay, well, maybe not *fail*, but I won't be able to be get an A."

"So? When you die, your tombstone isn't going to say, 'Lily Drummond. B in Lit Study.' I feel like you'll survive."

"This is so ridiculous. I know everything about Elinor. Ask me. I don't have time to rewrite this whole thing because she wants me to try something new. There is absolutely nothing wrong with doing what's familiar. Why does everyone want things to be different all the time anyway?"

Kristen reaches over and takes the paper out of my hand and tears it up. It's a symbolic gesture; the original is saved on my laptop and I've memorized my professor's comments. Still, I actually reach for the flickering scraps, ready to tape them back together only to be reminded of how shallow I am.

"Write something else," she tells me.

"I can't."

"Then go for a walk. And when you come back, come back ready to start over. There's nothing wrong with starting over. People do it all the time."

Arguing with her is pointless, because people like her do. People like Kristen come away to college and make friends while grabbing a pizza menu in the lounge and shed who they used to be like another skin they've outgrown. But for people like me, the past is a guide to the future, a lesson in how many mistakes you've made and how to be better. Otherwise, it's just a cycle of screwing up over and over again and that terrifies me.

Rocks were complicated. I wouldn't have thought so, but I'd studied for weeks because there were just too many kinds of rocks. I didn't understand all the variations in rocks and how they were formed, but I kept making the flashcards. It didn't stick, but I didn't have much of a choice. I had never done poorly on anything. I was only ten, but rocks would be the death of me.

'Explain the difference between slate and shale.' I'd stared at the question for half the exam. I had been almost certain one was sedimentary, but I didn't know which – and the other could have been anything. I knew these had to have been in my notes and on my flashcards, but after a while, the words became little dancing letters on the page, as sensible as if the question had asked me about folk art of the indigenous people on

Neptune. They were words – something that had always been reliable – but these words were going to ruin me and I couldn't make sense of them.

It didn't surprise me, of course, when Mr. Grunyan came to my desk with my test paper folded over. We all knew what that fold meant. When you did well, no one hid the results. They were displayed in massive red ink next to a sticker, but when you failed… well, the hidden number or letter didn't matter because we all knew what the fold meant.

"You made a mistake," I said when he handed it to me, his eyes sad because I tried hard. I wasn't the kind of student a teacher wanted to see struggle, because I did my work and I paid attention and I never complained. But being polite doesn't mean you know shit about rocks.

"I'm sorry," he said and I believed him. The apology wasn't going to fix it, though. There, under the dreaded crease, was something I only imagined from books I'd read. At ten-years-old, you don't expect to see an F on a test, especially when you study. Three red scratches, but they were three scratches that screamed, 'you're not perfect.' And that wasn't an option.

"But-" I couldn't argue, though. I had wasted the exam time on shale and slate and left a bunch of answers blank and even several of the ones I did fill out were wrong. I had failed.

Failure was an abstract concept. I knew to fear it. I knew it meant I wasn't good enough and I knew that it would be some kind of record of that imperfection, but having never experienced it, I didn't really understand it. You only failed if you didn't try, if you didn't work hard enough, but to fail when you had done everything you could was something you could feel in your soul. Every doubt inside your head was confirmed in that one letter, because you knew someday you wouldn't be able to keep up and there it was, laid out like a bleeding injury on a white test page.

"I'm available after school this Thursday for retakes," Mr. Grunyan said. I was young and there were retakes still, but even if no one else knew, even if my parents didn't ask – although I knew they would – Mr. Grunyan and I would know.

"It's not that big of a deal," Jon said on the bus ride home, and it wasn't for him. He'd come home with bad grades, not to mention bruises from fighting and dirty

116

clothes and once he had brought home a note from a teacher because he'd cursed in class. But in the second grade, I had asked my teacher for chocolate milk instead of white milk once and she'd called my mom to verify that it was okay; I'd been punished for three weeks. I wasn't allowed snacks or to watch TV because "good girls don't ask questions. Good girls behave and do what they're told." It was about milk, but I had upset the process. I had tried to think for myself.

"She's going to kill me," I said.

"No, she won't. You might be grounded, but it's just one F and you can make it up."

But he was wrong. The makeup was irrelevant.

She asked as soon as she got home.

"Before you get upset," I started, but I didn't get to finish. She was in my bag and pulling the paper out, with its crease down the middle, staring at it. Her hand shook as she clutched it, watching it and waiting for the letter to change. "I can make it up," I offered.

I think I could've handled it if she had yelled at me, if she'd turned to me and given me a lecture. I could have made up the test and I would've tried even harder, but when she did turn to look at me, there was nothing in

117

her eyes. She looked at me like she couldn't believe she had ever hoped for anything from me and then she threw the paper at me. It didn't hurt; it was paper after all. But she threw it aside and looked at me like I was as meaningless as a creased test. She said nothing at all, shaking her head, and leaving me alone in the room with the disappointment.

I did make up the test and I got an A, after seeing Mr. Grunyan for help and having him explain rocks in a different way, but it really didn't matter, because the failure never fades.

HOVERING

21.

I hate the fall. Now that the weather has finally caught up, it's freezing and all the trees are bare. It's only been a few days since I got back and yet fall just came in, blanketed the entire world in death, and then left things for us to mourn.

"You mind company?" Campus is dark but I don't have to turn around to recognize his voice. I don't stop walking and I don't turn around, but I shake my head as invitation.

"Fall is so depressing," he says when he's beside me. "Do we need an annual ceremony to remind us that everything ends?"

"I was just thinking the same thing."

We walk around the quad, not speaking, but it's pleasant. There's a faded light in the library windows and music is playing from some of the dorms, but it's all *away*. Both physically distant and almost surreal.

For nearly thirty minutes, we just walk, our breath meeting the chill in the air and the only sound outside of the echoes of dorm life are our shoes on the crunchy remnants of leaves.

"What brings you out here?" he finally asks, after we've circled the quad several times, but it's a question with no timeline. It takes another circle before I reply.

"I don't know. I'm just walking. I screwed up a paper and I don't know how to fix it and things just all seem to feel like they're out of control," I explain.

"You really do put a lot of stock in rules, don't you?"

I nod, but he catches it because he's looking. I like the way he looks at me. It's a curious look, but I've been struck before by his eyes and the depth of them that when he looks at me, I feel complex. Jack also has a sincerity in his look and I can't remember when – or if – someone looked at me like that last.

"What happens if you break them?" he asks.

"I don't."

"But if you did?"

I stop, the leaves resistant to my feet digging them into dust, and look away from the buildings with life in them, towards one of the academic halls that rests in darkness with only a sole security light to give it presence. I really hate the fall, because the smell of wood smoke and the crispness of cold make me want to love it. I want to picture Halloween and childhood and fireplaces and cocoa, but all I can think about is the fact that even the trees know nothing is permanent.

"When I was a kid, before... well, when I was really young, I loved to play in the woods," I say. "There was a massive forest behind my house. I mean, it probably wasn't massive at all, but when I was five, it felt it. My brother was just my brother and I wasn't a girl and he wasn't a boy and no one cared about appearances and rules. We used to stay out in the woods until it got dark – and then we would stay longer, just to see if we could. There was one night my dad came to get us, during the summer, and it was after dinner and his flashlight was the only thing that made the woods real, part of this world. I lived in my imagination in those woods and everything was possible."

Jack sits on the curb under the streetlight, but he doesn't interrupt. I join him, the cold concrete sneaking past my jeans, but it keeps me grounded. Memory feels a little too strong tonight. Fall does that.

"Eventually, I was told I couldn't go in the woods, because girls didn't do that and girls wore dresses and sat quietly and they behaved and they followed the rules."

"That's stupid," Jack says.

I laugh and it feels good. I can't remember the last time I laughed so naturally. "It is. But that's not the story."

"So tell me."

I rub my hands together and place them between my knees. It grows cold quickly in New England during autumn, but this is quiet and easy and I don't want to go inside. Not yet.

"There was one day. One day in high school. A year ago almost. It was right after my birthday, right after... well, it was a confusing time. And I came home from school and no one was there and I don't know why. I don't know what it was that day in particular, but I needed to go to the woods and I wanted them to be the same."

"Nothing ever stays the same. It's both the greatest comfort of life and the singular tragedy of it."

"Who said that?" I ask.

Jack laughs. "Fuck if I know. I think I did."

"Well, you should make that a thing."

"A thing?"

"A thing," I confirm. When he smiles, it's a simple smile, one that sneaks into your world before you can decide if you want to allow it, before you can decide if the other person deserves your smile. I want to deserve it. I don't know why. He's just a guy and I'm just a girl and it's fall and it's cold, but his smile lightens some of what I'm carrying.

"What happened in the woods?" he asks. He's watching me speak and it makes me uncomfortable, but in a way that I enjoy. He's listening and it's so new to have someone truly listen like this that I almost want to stop and ask what he wants in return. But I don't think I can handle it if there is a cost.

"You're right. It wasn't the same. It was November and the snow came suddenly and the trees were bare.

Plus I was eighteen and they weren't big and the woods weren't massive. I could see the neighbors on every end of the woods and instead of feeling lost and secure, I felt like I was being inspected." I pause and look up at the sky, but the lights from the street and the buildings washes out any stars.

"There was something new, though. Something about the trees," I continue. I can't believe I'm still talking and that he's interested. I pause again, because it sounds stupid, but he nods to encourage me to go on.

"I looked up at the sky and even though the woods had gotten small, the sky was still huge. It seemed endless and I tried to remember. I tried to picture it the way I remembered, but instead, I imagined a new version. Something that had never existed. I imagined woods and a lake and a clear sky with the moon and the stars. I could hear the owls crying. It all felt more real than everything I knew, and it was all in my head."

"It sounds beautiful," he says. "And there's nothing wrong with wanting to imagine beauty when the world seems to be lacking in it."

"You asked what happens if I break the rules, and here I am talking about trees."

"So? If it makes you happy, embrace it."

"Do you ever feel alone?" I ask.

He looks down and his breathing slows, as if it hurts to answer. Like he's trying to find the oxygen to reply. "In ways I don't think I'm ready to tell you about. I don't feel alone, Lily. I *am*."

"You used my name," I point out.

"Sorry. Should I go back to Elinor?"

I shake my head. "I don't think so. I think I've been living too long as Elinor. Maybe you were right the day we met. Maybe the real story is Marianne's."

"Or maybe it's not about someone else's story, Lily," he says and he stands. I don't want to go back yet, but it's freezing and the lights are going down in the dorms and library and it's getting dark. He reaches a hand out to help me up and I hold it longer than I should and longer than I need to, but neither of us mentions it.

"Thanks for walking with me, Jack," I say, and we make our way back to our dorm. As we cross from the quad into all the streams of light, the spell is broken, but it doesn't matter. Kristen was right; a walk was just what I needed.

****

Not sure what brings me there, I gather my laptop and copy of *Sense and Sensibility* and head to Jack's room. I didn't ask. I haven't seen him since last night and we didn't make any kind of promises, but I need to rewrite this paper and my mind felt open when I was talking to him, so I go in spite of it being odd. When he doesn't answer after I knock twice, though, I start to think I'm a moron.

"You could have at least checked with him before bringing your computer," I mumble to myself and I'm about to turn around when the door opens. He's dressed, but his eyes are heavy, almost like he's been sleeping. He stands in the space between the door and the room and takes in my full arms.

"Writing that paper?" he asks.

"Yeah. I'm sorry. This was stupid. I shouldn't have... I mean, I didn't think," I stutter.

"Hold on, okay?"

He shuts the door and I stand in the hallway, wondering if I should go back to my room as the minutes pass. I'm ready to leave when he opens the door again. This time, he opens it all the way and invites me in.

"Alana," he says, which I don't understand at first until he moves aside. The girl on his bed is beautiful, but not in the way you normally recognize someone as beautiful. It's not a physical beauty, but a sense that she has walked through the world and survived something awful. Grace, I guess people call it, but I've never seen it in person before.

"I'm sorry," I say. "I didn't realize you had company."

"I was just leaving," Alana replies. "Jack, I'll... call you, I guess."

He's just a guy – a guy who picked up a book for me. Our lives are not linked in any way. He owes me nothing, yet in some of the emptiest moments since I started school, he's been there. Coincidentally, sure, but he's been there. Yet as I watch Alana flip her long, dark hair up into a rubber band and she and Jack avoid looking at each other, I feel like an intruder not just in his private moment with her, but also in his life. They don't make eye contact at all and the silence in the moments between her getting off the bed and leaving lingers once the door is closed.

"I shouldn't have come." Breaking the silence seems almost sacrilegious, but the soft buzzing of Jack's overhead light is humming inside my brain. "I'm sorry. I interrupted something."

"It's nothing," he says finally and lifts his head.

The only guys I've really known, beyond quick conversations in class or as Abby's recent interests, are Jon and Derek. Since arriving at college, the illusions I've held about Derek are slowly peeling away, but they're still the precedent for guys in general for me. So seeing Jack in pain bothers me. It changes my perceptions and I don't do well with that. My own agony is something I bury as much as I can, but I gather that mine is only the superficial flaking off of what I see in him. And it terrifies me to feel so helpless.

"I never asked," I comment. "I told you I had a boyfriend, but I never asked about her. I should've asked."

"She's not my girlfriend." He stresses this fact like it's absolutely necessary that I recognize it as truth. "Not for a long time."

"But she was?"

He opens his window and takes out a pack of cigarettes. I don't like the smell of smoke, but he's trying to hold his hands steady while he gets the cigarette out and I worry he'll light himself on fire with the way he can't control the lighter. I'm about to offer to help when he gets it lit and tosses the lighter onto his dresser. He sits on his bed, smoothing down the covers, and takes a long drag on his cigarette, not answering my question and not looking at me. We're definitely not supposed to be smoking in the dorms.

"Last night, you asked me if I ever feel alone. There are things I spend most of my time trying to keep distant, to leave in the past and let go, but yes, I do. I feel that way a lot. In high school, I had two friends – Alana and Dave. And now..." He stops and finishes his cigarette. I don't push him, because he'll tell me, but I want him to be ready. I just want to be able to listen.

He doesn't close the window when he's done, but he does look at me. "Dave's overseas."

"Traveling?" I think of Abby and her Europe adventures. She sends me emails once a week and texts when she can, but I miss talking to her. She keeps promising we'll Skype, but then something always comes up.

"Army. He's in Afghanistan."

"Oh." Of course he is. My friend is sitting in cafes in Paris and eating gelato in Rome, while Jack's friend is fighting a war most of us have forgotten exists.

"We stopped talking before he left, though. He didn't want to go and die and leave us missing him, so he just cut us out of his life. It really sucked."

"I can imagine."

"Can you?" he asks. It's a question that could be cruel, judgmental, or damning, but he's merely curious. And he's right. I can't imagine. I say I can and I have my own secrets and fears, but I can already tell Jack and I come from very different places.

"Never mind," he says. "Anyway, yeah, it was just the three of us for a long time. Maybe one of these days I'll tell you the story, although trust me, it's better just not talking about it. After a few years, I got used to the idea that everyone assumes a lot of things because of who I am."

"Well, then, everyone's stupid. You're only who you decide you are."

Jack laughs. "Funny. I feel like you've never believed that yourself."

I feel weird standing in the middle of his dorm room, but he doesn't have an extra bed and there's a stack of books on his chair. I look between them and the corner of his bed, debating if I should just move the books.

"I don't bite. It's only a shitty dorm room cot, but I think there's enough room," he says.

I sit with him, leaning against the wall and he closes the window when he sees me shiver. Figures that fall decided just to skip right to winter in a day. In a year when I need change to happen gradually, it just happens in an instant.

"I only had one real friend," I tell him.

"That surprises me," he admits.

"Why?"

"I don't know. I think I assumed a lot of things about you when I met you, but you deserve better than that. I'm sorry."

I shrug. "I don't think I'm a full person. It's hard not to assume, when I don't even know what's real."

"Don't feel like you need to explain. If you want to, I'll listen, but you owe me nothing."

"Thank you," I reply.

"There's nothing to thank me for. It's just decency," he says. There's a deep break in the conversation and I don't know if I should confess or if I should push for his story, but it passes and he turns on the lamp on his dresser and starts his laptop.

"What brought you here anyway?" Jack asks.

"I need to work on my paper."

"So you came here?"

"I guess." I can't explain why. I can't even explain it to myself.

"All right then. Get writing."

"What are you going to do?" I ask him.

"I have no idea. You just showed up with a laptop and a book," he reminds me.

"Tell me your story, Jack. Tell me about Alana."

"Another time. You want something to drink?" He gets up and goes to a small fridge near his wardrobe. I expect a beer, since I feel like drinking is synonymous with college, but he only has cranberry juice. It's so ridiculous that I start laughing and he stares at me. "Something funny?"

"No, I just wasn't expecting you to have juice. Especially cranberry."

"Looks like we're both shaking some assumptions, aren't we?"

"Seems to be." I take the bottle of cranberry juice and turn on my computer. For two hours, Jack works on something on his computer on the end of his bed by the window and I sit across from him with my own. I consider revising my essay on Elinor, but I think about the rules and expectations and what my professor said and then I start new. After all, like Kristen said, what's the worst that could happen?

22.

Kayla didn't let the book contest go. When the new girl moved into town at the end of the year and started in our class, I was introduced as "Lily, but don't talk to her because she cheats and she's think she's better than everyone." She was wrong, because I didn't think I was better than anyone at all; I wasn't even good enough to be me. But truth is rarely more than the right combination of words at the right time.

No one in our class had opinions except Kayla. Whenever a teacher would ask a question, Kayla answered and everyone agreed. She lived in the biggest house in town and her mother was French and baked treats and wore designer clothes and her father worked in the city. These were all things that impressed us at nine, because they impressed our parents and we were all still extensions of what we had learned at home. So when Mr. Chaves, our art teacher, came to our reading *class for a "cross-curricular lesson," and he asked us to describe our favorite illustrated books, Kayla said <u>The Polar Express.</u> We assumed that this was the collective answer, because Kayla had decreed it. It was a good book, so I didn't mind really, even though my favorite was actually <u>The Velveteen Rabbit</u>.*

"I love Maurice Sendak," the new girl added. "<u>Where the Wilds Thing Are</u> is wonderful."

The whole class looked at her. This wasn't how things were done. A teacher asked, Kayla answered, and we agreed. If a teacher called on someone else, we waited until Kayla had made it clear what she thought before we offered anything. So when the new girl gave a secondary option, Mr. Chaves was excited. I imagined teachers preferred to hear variety, but none of us knew how to handle it. There was Kayla's opinion and that was all. Kayla, of course, was not excited and she glared at the new girl.

"I said <u>The Polar Express</u>," she reiterated.

"Great. And that's your favorite, but there's more than one book," the other girl replied.

I didn't like Kayla. She had been mean to me about the contest and although I liked <u>The Polar Express </u>and

I was too afraid to say anything to contradict her, I hadn't forgotten about it, either. I also didn't forget the way she'd gloated at the Easter egg hunt. My dad had told me it wasn't nice when I called her a stupid cow at dinner that night and I'd tried to be nice after that, but I couldn't help getting pleasure from watching her face turn red now that someone else had an idea.

"Listen, new girl," Kayla snapped.

"Abby. My name is Abby. It's not hard to remember. It's four letters."

Kayla sputtered and her face looked like a violent tomato. I had to try not to giggle, because it made me happy to see someone argue with Kayla. I always wished I had fought back when she spread lies about me.

"I was nice to you. I warned you about her," Kayla said to Abby and she pointed her finger in my direction. I was her nemesis, even though neither of us could spell the word and we wouldn't know what it meant for another year. I never actually figured out why I had earned that privilege, besides beating her at something, but it served me well with Abby.

"Yes, you did, but Lily is my best friend, so you can just shut up."

Abby took her things and moved to sit next to me and she put her arm around my shoulders to confirm that we were, in fact, best friends. Years later, we laughed about the silliness of it all, but that day, it was a battle and Abby intended to win. After Kayla moved away before high school, Abby and I were still close, all because a grudge about the reading contest had brought us together.

For the rest of the day, Abby followed me around and all week, whenever she would see Kayla, she would laugh as if I'd told a fantastic joke. I didn't know any jokes and it took a while before I told Abby much of anything at all, but she became my friend that day because it made her mad that everyone else ostracized me. That ended up being what kept us close as we got older. Although I wasn't interesting to ostracize by high school, Abby always felt like the only person who cared.

The following week, we were asked to read aloud from the books we were currently reading, and Kayla's hand went up – obviously. But so did Abby's. Miss Stephens, taken aback, called on Abby, because it was a voice she'd never heard. Kayla, shocked, slammed her book down.

"I'm telling my parents," she announced.

"Kayla, you can read, too," Miss Stephens said. "Abby's just going to go first."

"I always go first," Kayla argued.

"Exactly, which is why we're letting Abby go today. Everyone deserves a chance, right, Kayla?"

As mean as Kayla was to me, she wouldn't contradict a teacher, so she sulked while Abby read and then Hannah went and several other kids read before she had her chance. Miss Stephens didn't falter, despite Kayla's loud sighs and complaints from her desk right up front. By the time she got to read, it was almost recess and no one was listening anymore and I was admittedly vindicated that Kayla could experience what it felt like to have your voice not matter.

At recess, she came over to me and Abby. We were sitting on a rock and talking about Abby's aunt's new puppy.

"You're not invited to use my pool," Kayla declared. This was the ultimate small town punishment, and she announced it with the full force of a judge meting out a sentence. Abby looked up at her, standing over us and

trying to be intimidating, although she was just another nine-year-old girl.

"That's okay," she replied. "I live on the lake and it's much bigger than your stupid pool anyway."

Kayla didn't know what to say, because no one had ever declined her mom's cookies or her pool invitations. Those were the things that made her powerful in elementary school, but Abby went back to the story of Buster, the Pomeranian, and ignored Kayla's further attempts to establish dominance. By the time recess ended, Kayla had been dethroned, but all efforts to set up Abby in her place went ignored as well. She just wanted to tell someone a story about a dog.

23.

Now that winter has shown its face, there's an unspoken transition on campus. The airiness of the first month and a half of school is replaced almost overnight with focus. Everyone shifts from making friends and creating plans to following through and giving up. It was only a few weeks ago when all the tables were out for the club fair and groups of people were listening to music, playing hackey sack, and acting as if school were an afterthought. But with the cold, the light cotton of summer gives way to tweed, and earnestness settles.

Of course I feel like I'm lagging behind the tide, but it's a space that's inherent and the catchup doesn't take as long. For me, the biggest change is the slow friendship I'm forming with Jack. Aside from his last name – Connelly – I haven't learned much more about him, but he's been helping with my paper and I spend my evenings studying in his room. I love the way I never have to work at anything around him, but I also worry that I'm just filling my life with him to avoid figuring out all I ever felt with Derek. I don't want our friendship to be a replacement for something else. It's only been two weeks since Columbus Day. It amazes me that two weeks in college can feel so much like a lifetime.

"I have band practice tonight," Jack says. We're in the cafeteria, although I haven't felt like eating much lately. I can still hear my mother talking about my weight and every bite of food makes me nauseous.

"That's okay. I need to finish my paper and I should go to the library. Research and stuff."

"Ah, yes, stuff."

I nod. "Stuff."

"Do you... do you want to do something this weekend?" he asks.

"Like a date?" It hurts to swallow when I say that. I don't want to confuse this. I'm enjoying Jack's company, but the idea of dating anyone – especially with the still present Derek problem – makes me want to run until I can't recognize anyone.

"Don't you have a boyfriend?"

"I don't know."

"You don't know?"

"We broke up," I say. "Sort of."

"Oh. You haven't mentioned it."

"Well, it's not a breakup. Maybe. We're on a break. He needs time or something. But we have plans in a couple weeks. For my birthday. So I don't know." It all sounds ridiculous when said aloud and I'm angry at Derek all over again.

"Okay, then. Well, not a date anyway. There's something I want to show you, but it would be one hell of a shitty date."

"Yeah, I'm free," I say.

"Can I ask you something?" he asks.

He's barely eating, which I notice since I've been rebuttering a piece of toast since we sat down, trying to appear interested in being here, but he keeps watching my knife slather the yellow spread onto the soggy slice and his dinner is getting cold.

"Ask away."

"Do you ever say no?"

"What do you mean?"

143

"I mean you don't know me. You don't know if I plan to take you out into a field somewhere and do horrible things to you."

"Do you?"

"God, no. But I mean, you come to my room with no fear, yet you rarely offer an opinion. You nod and agree, but in the short time I've known you, you seem to spend a lot of time saying yes and very little arguing."

"Not everything needs to be an argument," I point out. "And I've snapped at you plenty."

"About Marianne and Elinor. About abstract concepts, but it's okay to say no."

"Why does it matter? It just upsets people when you're contrary and you haven't given me a reason to treat you that way."

He takes a bite of his pasta finally. I can almost feel the slimy noodles in my throat, but I'm getting fat. I salivate watching him eat the cold cafeteria pasta. Flipping over the heavily buttered bread, I start on the back side.

"I wasn't kidding when I told you I had only two friends," he says. "And all three of us are beyond

144

fucked up. I'm not a good person. You should just know that, before you agree to do anything with me at all. There are things in a person's life that you can't stop knowing once you learn them."

I think I'm a selfish person. At no point has Jack benefitted from knowing me. I go to his room and we talk and I do homework, but I don't encourage him to talk about his life. He makes vague references and says he's uncomfortable, and I allow that to be enough, but it's also me. All I've done is think about what I did wrong to upset Derek, about my mom and how she would judge Jack, and about what I can do to be better and to put my life back in order the way it used to be.

"I'm sure you're not a bad person," I tell him, but we both know I'm lying. I'm not sure of anything. I'm not even sure what kind of person I am.

"Tell me about your boyfriend," he invites. "Or your not boyfriend."

I want to eat my nasty bread slice, but it's too heavy now. I watch Jack spin spaghetti around his fork and it hurts inside of me, in my bones even, but my mom said I had gotten fat and Derek broke up with me and the pasta is to blame.

"What about him?"

"What's his name?" he asks.

Maybe he'd let me taste just the sauce.

I peel the soggy crust off of the bread, careful not to get any of the butter on it before I eat it. I don't know what I was thinking. I wanted to look normal, like I was readying myself to eat it, but now it's a Day-Glo yellow square in the middle of a cracked plastic plate. That feels like a metaphor.

"Derek," I reply. Jack's watching me pretend to eat, but he says nothing.

"What kind of guy is Derek? Does he read Jane Austen, too? Does he hate the fall or like the security of trees?"

It's really strange how things happen. In the same sudden spark that makes you fall in love, you find yourself out of it. What a quiet, rainy summer day created suddenly explodes in a question that digs all the way through me.

24.

"That's stupid," Derek said.

"Okay, we don't have to. It was just an idea."

It was his Spring Break and the snow had melted. He was supposed to come over as soon as he got home, but it was Monday and he'd been busy and I'd missed him. When he'd asked what I wanted to do, I thought about us and our beginnings and I'd suggested driving up to New Hampshire, to the campground where I fell in love with him, but he was right. It was stupid. The ground was still frozen and the air retained its chill even though the sun was blooming. It was a long ride to sit on icy soil, but after a few months, we still didn't have anything that was ours – except that one afternoon.

"Gas is crazy expensive."

"It's fine," I agreed. "You're right."

"And it's cold as fuck outside."

"I know. I agree. Like I said, it was just an idea."

"Look, Lily, it's an okay idea in theory and I appreciate the thought, but let's be honest that it's dumb. Some dirt and trees aren't why I love you and we don't need to make things complicated and inconvenient and stupid to prove a point."

I nodded, but it was hard not to cry. He was right, sure, but he didn't need to call it stupid.

We ended up going to a movie. I couldn't focus on it. It was something about a spy and a missing bomb or something. Derek had picked it. It didn't matter. I sat in the dark theatre and for two hours, I merely tried to keep in the tears.

Since I'd slept with him, we were a couple, but I'd spent more nights crying and lonely than I had in the years before. Maybe it was just the disappointment of expectation, waiting for him to call only for him to send me a text after 11 telling me he was too busy to chat and he'd call the next day.

He sat in the movie, shoving popcorn into his mouth and ignoring me completely unless he needed me to hand him the soda, and never thought about what he'd said. He said it, we didn't discuss it, and it had passed. I knew that if I brought it up, he would tell me to stop *being difficult, that it wasn't a big deal, that I needed to stop holding a grudge. He always said things like that when he was careless with his words. And they were only words after all.*

"Are you parents home?" Derek asked after the movie was over. I think the spy had found the bomb. I knew he'd met some girl spy and they'd had a lot of sex, and then someone drove a car off a bridge, but I didn't remember the bomb.

I looked at my watch. It was only 2:30 and they wouldn't be home until at least six. I shook my head. "Not for a while."

"What about Jon? He had said he was doing something today?"

"No, there's no one home."

He smiled and kissed the top of my head. "So I'm coming over?"

Although he asked it like a question, I knew that it was a decree. "I guess."

"What's wrong?" He was irritated and he couldn't hide it. He crushed the cup of soda in his hand and crumbled the popcorn bag. I followed him as he stomped heavily down the cinema stairs into the hallway. When

149

we got to the car, he turned around and looked at me finally. I had to run to catch up.

"Why do you always make things complicated?" he asked. "You always make a big deal out of dumb things like a campsite and then the whole day is ruined. Why can't you just be fun? I want a fun girlfriend."

"I'm sorry. I wasn't trying to. You can come over." I wanted to tell him that sometimes I wanted more from our relationship. Sometimes I thought a boyfriend would talk to you, would express interest in you as a person. But I knew it was because of me. I wasn't pretty enough. I wasn't fun. I didn't know how to be a girlfriend, because I tried so hard and although he said he loved me, he didn't understand why the campsite mattered to me. That had to be my fault.

He opened my car door and when we were inside, he kissed me and ran his hands over my hair, before letting them slide down my body. He reached one between my legs, not doing more than tapping his fingers against my thigh, but he groaned when he did, his kiss becoming more aggressive until I was pushed against the car window and trying not to suffocate.

"God, Lily. Are you mad because of how you make me feel?"

"No, I'm not mad."

"You should be flattered. I can't control how attracted to you I am, because you're just so sexy. Don't be upset that I love you so much it's all I think about. I can't stop thinking about how much I love what we do."

"I love you, too," I whispered.

"Good. Let's get going. I need some quality alone time with you badly."

My mom still decorated my room and she hadn't seemed to acknowledge that I was a high school senior and technically an adult. It's bad enough to lose your virginity when your family is nearby, or for your relationship to exist mainly in a backseat, but there is something damning about a grown man heaving and thrusting on top of you while you try to ignore the fact that your teddy bear is still under your ass and if he doesn't slow down, he's going to knock the cartoon cat pictures right down onto his sweaty, red face.

Derek grunted and made noises and I pressed my hand against the singing Calico above to stop it from falling.

"You're so sexy," he said again when he finished.

He'd never told me I was beautiful or smart or kind. Just sexy. Always sexy. I didn't feel sexy. I felt sad and every time I felt sadder, but I didn't want to feel that way. I loved him. Sex with a boy you love shouldn't make you empty and sad.

25.

Kristen went out with Lyle, so when Jack comes to get me on Saturday morning, I'm rereading *Sense and Sensibility.* I only have a few more days to get things down for my paper and I'm trying to make sense of Marianne, but her passions and values are so conflicted with everything I know. When Jack knocks loudly, I answer as soon as I hear it, yet he's already halfway back down the hall when I open the door.

"Jack?" I call after him.

He turns, shoving his cell phone in his pocket. "This was a bad idea," he says. "I wanted to tell you, to explain, but I can't. I can't bear it."

"No. I said I wanted to go. I want to hear it."

"You don't," he argues.

"I do, and I'm arguing with you. Like you asked. Don't walk away. Wait here. I'm grabbing my coat. We have plans," I tell him.

I wonder if he'll actually wait while I turn off my computer and find a coat and shoes, but he does. He's still standing in the middle of the hallway while people pass in and out of their rooms around him. The sterile walls and floor are endless white and Jack, in his dark clothes, looks like a bad image from a cheesy horror movie. But when I reach him, he just looks scared.

I thought we were going to go to a park or the river or something, so when Jack pulls into the visitor parking lot of the prison, I keep my mouth shut and follow him. It's sunny even though it's cold, but around the building, the light feels diluted, short bursts of sunlight trapped in the barbed wire circling the area. There's a guard tower to the left and I can see someone in there; I don't know if it's only in movies where they stand there with loaded guns and keep an eye out for trouble, but either way, it's intimidating. I can't imagine being here at all, but when we go through the guard post inside and he knows them all by first name, I realize he's spent a lot of time here. What kind of life is it to be a regular visitor at a state prison by the time you're twenty?

After we get through security, we're led through another massive door and I'm surprised when Jack takes my hand. I'm sure it's as much for me as it is for him, but the tension in his grip is heartbreaking. I barely know him, but the pain I feel knowing that this is a part of his secret and his own self-hate doesn't have to be logical.

Inside the open room where we're told to wait, there are three gray tables. Jack chooses the one by the window, although it's not much of a window. Too high and too small to let in much more than a sliver of light, it's like a taunt to the men locked up in here – a memory of a world that exists beyond them and has forgotten them.

"Don't go feeling bad," Jack says next to me while we wait. He taps his foot and the anxiety reaches out of him like a creeping plant that suffocates everything in its path. "For me or for anyone in here."

"How'd you know?" I ask.

"I can see it in your eyes. You look sad and sympathetic, but you don't end up here for small mistakes, Lily. You end up here because you decided the world deserved to suffer."

"I still don't understand why you think-"

I don't get to finish. His eyes are drawn towards the door, where a man in his early 40's is being led towards us by two guards. His hair is too long and he hasn't shaved in some time. Gaunt and weak, he needs to rely on the guards to bring him to the chair and they stand over him while he sits. He's still cuffed. As he lifts his head, I see the resemblance immediately. He and Jack have the same eyes. However, where Jack's are full of light, this man is only darkness. If it were possible for eyes to be totally hollow, his would be.

"It's been a while," the man says to Jack.

"Two weeks."

"I can't remember the last time you came alone."

"For good reason. I changed my mind. We're going."

Jack gets up and knocks over the metal chair. He doesn't force me up but he waits for me to stand. I want to disappear because this is too intimate and Jack was right; I don't belong here. Not because I don't want to be a part of it or because I feel differently about him, but because this is private and I don't warrant this kind of trust.

I slide out past Jack, but then wait. He's not moving, just staring at the man.

"You can't hate me forever," he says to Jack. He looks up at his son, but Jack keeps his gaze on the door.

"I don't know. I think maybe I can," he replies.

"Someday, you're going to have to listen."

"There is nothing you can say," Jack spits back and then we're leaving. He doesn't take my hand this time, but he does stop once we pass security to make sure I'm with him, and then when we get outside, he collapses back against the prison wall.

"I'm sorry," he says. "I shouldn't have done this. I thought I would be okay. I thought I could tell you and it wouldn't hurt. I avoid it because it always hurts."

I join him, leaning against the wall, and watch the clouds settle over the sun. It's one of those days when the universe seems to get it.

"Let's get out of here," he says. "Want to see where I live?"

I nod, but in the two hours it takes to get to his house, we don't speak at all. I know he's afraid I'm judging him, but I don't have the right words to tell him that it's so far from that. I just want to be worthy of a story like Jack's.

The small, faded green house is set at the end of a long dirt road with a yard that's mostly dirt as well, although there are a few patches of overgrown grass where the dirt didn't win. A rusted tricycle rests against the metal fence that Jack opens, and he leads me up the steps and in to the house. The shingles are falling loose from the roof and the gutters are clogged with leaves. Inside, an old woman is sitting on a broken couch, reading a book. She looks up when we come in.

"This is Lily," Jack says. "My grandmother," he explains to me, but there is no formal introduction. She just nods and goes back to her book and he leads me downstairs into the basement. A small room off the main room appears to be his. It doesn't look much different from his dorm room, except that there's more stuff. It's also somehow more sterile, even though there are posters on the walls and clothes and junk strewn everywhere.

"So, this is my shit life," he tells me. "And that's what I become."

"What? What's what you become?"

"My dad. A man in prison. Worthless."

"You're right. I saw a man in a prison," I tell him. "I don't know why he was there or what you think it means for you. But I definitely don't think you automatically become anything, regardless."

"You know, maybe if he'd robbed a convenience store or sold drugs or something, it would be different. But what he did… it doesn't go away."

"What did he do?" I don't know if I should ask, but curiosity gets the better of me.

"He murdered my mother. In front of me."

For all of my understanding that people have different stories and backgrounds, everyone I know is basically the same. I don't come from a world where things like this happen anywhere but in movies or on the nightly news. There is nothing I can say, nothing I can do. My entire sense of reality, of what's normal, implodes around me; the fragile shards of my ignorance cut me deeply. I tell myself I need to say something – anything – but I can't find the words. Jack looks at me, though, his eyes so sad, and I want to try. I want desperately to try. I just don't know how.

"You don't have to tell me," I say, "but you can. I'll listen."

"Are you sure? Do you really want to know?"

"I want to be your friend," I say. "I want you to let me."

He nods, sits back down on the bed, and starts talking. "When I was little, my parents fought like crazy. I didn't understand drugs when I was a kid. I knew my mom drank, but that was the only thing I saw. Except her arms. I knew about her arms, but I was a kid. None of us knew why she looked like that, although everyone's parents knew and that made things hard. They didn't really want a junkie's kid at Chuck E Cheese with their children.

"Dad worked a lot. He was never home. He probably had a girlfriend somewhere, but again, these are things you don't know when you're younger. But when he came home, it was terrible. I remember one time Mom was strung out or something and she wouldn't get off the couch. I didn't know why and I couldn't get her to get up. Dad kept telling her that she needed to, to do something, to feed me. It was the summer and I'd been wearing the same clothes for days. I ate when my friends' parents invited me over for lunch, the few who felt bad enough for me that they tried to intervene. At seven and eight, it never occurred to me that they looked at me with pity.

"I thought it was great when my dad wasn't around, because when my friends had to go in for dinner or go take a bath, I could just stay out all night playing. I used to hate it when he came home. He would always make me clean up and he would give me a curfew."

He pauses, but I don't speak. I don't think he wants anything but someone to listen to him right now. His hands knot the bed sheet and he tries to remain stoic.

"So he'd come home and it was summer and she wouldn't get up. He kept screaming, but she just wouldn't move. I offered to help and she ignored me. My dad ignored me and continued to berate her. Eventually, she started to laugh, and he picked her up and threw her out into the driveway. Literally threw her, like trash. She landed on the ground and I thought she had twisted something, but she just sat on the ground, laughing. My dad told her not to come back until she got her shit together and I didn't see her for the rest of the summer.

"Eventually, the cops brought her back to us. She didn't look any different and she didn't get her shit together, but my father had no idea what to do. Nothing changed. She didn't even make empty promises that they would. We just went right back into the routine. Dad tried at first to stay home more, but then he almost lost his job. My grandmother offered to help and to look after me when he couldn't. If it wasn't for her, who knows what would've happened? Dad worked, Mom got high, and I was just in the way."

"She's your dad's mother?" I ask.

He shakes his head. "My mother's. But everyone knew what my mom had become. She wanted to help, since she couldn't help her own daughter. Everyone in town knew, everyone at church knew, everyone at school knew. Everyone except me. Even if they'd tried to explain it to me, I wouldn't have understood. I still loved her, despite it all. I didn't know any better. I just knew she was my mom. You have to love your mom, right?"

"I don't know how to answer that," I tell him. "Maybe another day."

"Yeah, that makes sense."

"Do you want to tell me about... when it happened?" I ask.

"You got to understand - that was just one time," he says. "It was always like that. All my memories are some version of that mess. She did something and ended up high and when he came home, he freaked out and threatened her, but nothing ever changed. I don't know. Maybe it was inevitable what he did, but she was still my mom. I loved her. I *still* love her, and he took her away from me. You don't forgive certain things."

"Who said you have to?" I ask.

He sighs. "Everyone. But it's easy to say, isn't it? It's easy to forgive theoretically, but they weren't there. If they hated each other, why didn't he just leave?"

He gets up and turns on music. It's not loud and I can't even make out the song, but I get that he needs to do something, to move, to keep himself grounded in the present while he works through telling me this. I prefer to keep my own memories to myself, too, but they seem stupid right now.

"The last time," Jack says, "I was fourteen. It was the same thing as always. I mean, it wasn't like that day was somehow worse, until it was. By then, I'd learned to take care of myself so my grandmother wasn't around as much. Mom still did nothing. Dad came home after being gone for almost a month and she was a mess. They fought, but they always fought. I was sitting in the living room and doing homework and trying not to listen, trying to tune out the screams and the cruelty they flung at each other. I don't know what changed for him. I don't know why it was different.

"Their fight became more violent than normal. Hitting each other had never been out of the question, but this was something else. I don't even really know who started it, but eventually, he stopped it. I was trying to learn about ions and then he was choking her. She stared at me and I think it was the only time I remember after a certain point when I believed she saw me. She looked at me and her eyes were asking me to help her, but I couldn't. I was too small, too scrawny, and I screamed and pleaded with him. I begged him to stop, but he just kept holding her down while she faded out, and then he snapped her neck in the middle of the living room. I saw the entire thing and there was nothing I could do. After that, I came to live here with my grandmother for good. I still freak out about ions."

"I'm sorry." It's a weak thing to say, but it's true and it's the only way to express how I feel about what he's gone through.

"Yeah. I hear that a lot," he says.

I'm about to say something else when he looks at me and his eyes break my heart. In them, I see that little boy – the dirty eight-year-old who didn't understand why his mommy left him all summer. I see the teenager who couldn't save his mother, not only from his dad but also from her own destruction. And I see the man he's becoming. I see this guy who has every reason to be angry, who could have been cruel when we met or at least closed himself off. He's still hurting inside but he's kind in a way I have never experienced.

"I don't want to end up like him," he says.

"You won't."

"What makes you so sure?" he asks.

I shake my head. "I don't know. I barely know you. I know that you are facing demons that I can't even imagine outside of a bad movie. I know that you're scared and that you aren't really sure about letting me in, but I also know that you genuinely cared when it was late and I was lonely. You didn't have to sit and have coffee with me that night. You didn't have to walk in circles around campus and talk about fall. You certainly didn't have to help me with my essay or invite me here, but you did. You've been my friend."

"You know," he says. "When I moved out here, I had to start high school all over again. So, that meant that not only was I the new kid, but I was also the killer's kid. High school sucks and it's bad enough for regular people. It's unbearable for people like me. People shunned me and, worse, there were those who didn't. They used to remind me every day of what I was. It took me forever to make friends. I had two for the rest of high school. Two friends. I couldn't wait to get away, to go to college, to not be that kid anymore."

"Has it helped?"

"College?" he asks. I nod. "Helped with what?"

"With escape."

"Yes and no," he admits. "On campus, I have school, the band, and even a few friends. Well, acquaintances. I still have to try not to get close to them, though, because I know what will happen if they find out. So, it's escape, but I always need to be on guard."

"I found out and I'm still here. I'm sure most people would give you a chance."

"Percentages seem to dictate otherwise," he says.

I feel sad for him, for what he's been through, for the way he's been treated. I know he doesn't want my pity, but I can't help it. It's just so much to put on someone so young. "There will always be people like Dave and Alana," I say.

"And you?"

"And me."

"I worked so hard in high school," he says. "Grades became everything, because if I did the work, I could get a scholarship and get out. Never underestimate the value of homework, I guess."

I can't help but laugh. Our worlds are vastly different, but in this way, we are exactly the same. "I still have to figure out Marianne and all her drama," I say, since my paper is sitting on my laptop, incomplete. I have always loved the novel, but now I feel ironically connected to it more than ever. However, my professor isn't going to care how relevant it is if I don't get my shit together and write about it.

"We can head back soon. You can come over? To write the paper?"

"Yeah. How'd you get a single anyway?" I ask.

"The university doesn't want the legal obligation of explaining to some kid's parents that they paired him with a convict's kid. I didn't really want a roommate anyway and I requested a single. Turns out it works well for everyone." *Good thing you asked about that,* I admonish myself.

"Does it get lonely?"

"Not having a roommate?" he asks.

"Yeah," I say, thinking of Kristen. I feel like she was crucial in getting me through the homesickness and sadness that filled my days at the beginning of the semester. Although maybe Jack didn't have anything to miss.

He shrugs. "Sometimes, but I'm good at lonely. It's easier not to see the way people look at you."

"They're missing out."

"Come on, Elinor. Let's get you back on track. You don't need this nonsense."

I don't argue with him and we head back to school, the conversation light – music, TV, classes – but I can't help feeling like everything in my world is different because of him. Where he thinks something is wrong with him, that people believe the worst, I just see someone who has made me feel normal. I see a guy who makes me feel more like myself than I've ever felt with anyone.

26.

My parents didn't really fight. Everyone else's did, but mine got along. All the time. The only "discussions" they ever had involved me, because my dad felt my mom was too hard on me. But she wanted me to be better. She meant well and I needed it. I needed to be better. To be perfect.

When you're young, you don't think of your parents as people and it wasn't until I was in high school that I understood what it was like to feel betrayed by someone you trusted. Like I said, they didn't fight, but they did have passive aggressive conversations that I didn't pick up on until I understood nuance. So even when I witnessed it in middle school, it didn't register as an argument. It was just who they were.

It was the summer after freshman year. One of those stupid days that was too hot to do anything and no one was going anywhere. Except my dad, because he had to work. Since my mom was a guidance counselor, she had more time off in the summer. Everyone thought she was always off, but that wasn't true. Still, she was home more, so Jon, my mom, and I were trying to clean because at least there was central air. Dad had said he might be late for a meeting or something and Jon was already complaining that he was hungry.

"I don't want to wait until he gets home. Why can't I just eat something now?" he asked my mother. She'd just come upstairs from the laundry room and was carrying a basket of clothes. It was a casual afternoon and there was nothing extraordinary about my mom doing laundry. When Jon asked about dinner, though, she lost it. She threw the laundry basket across the kitchen, socks and underwear freefalling around the appliances, and then she slammed the basement door.

"Do what you want. Who cares? You'll do it anyway, won't you?"

Jon didn't know what he'd said, but he stopped asking about food and grabbed a granola bar before disappearing into his room. He muttered something about women being crazy as he went and my mom threw a plate after him, which shattered against the wall.

My mother never broke. She was perfect. She smiled and she said the right things and did the right things and everyone listened to her, but I was trapped behind the island in the kitchen, where I'd been filling a glass of water, and I had no idea what to do. I didn't think she even saw me standing there when she collapsed onto the floor, crying. My brain was telling me to get out, but my heart broke watching her cry. I didn't want anyone throwing a plate at me, but then again, I couldn't walk away. I hated her for so many reasons, but I couldn't watch her cry and not hurt.

"Are you okay?" I asked, which was stupid but there aren't a lot of ways to address your crying mother.

"You need to work harder, Lily. You can't let them down."

"Who?"

She looked up at me and handed me something. It was a small locket and there was nothing inside of it. Silver that was scratched from running through the dryer and no chain. I didn't know what I was supposed to do with it. "Who am I letting down?" I repeated.

172

She didn't answer. She looked at me and at the locket in my hand and then she stood up, cleaned the clothes and broken pieces of plate, and put everything away. For the next three hours, I followed her around and helped her clean the house because her emotions were scaring me, but I had no idea what to say or do about them. We ended up eating peanut butter and jelly sandwiches I made in the darkened kitchen when it came time for dinner.

My father made it home a little after nine. Jon hadn't come back down at all and I was still sitting with my mom at the table. I'd picked up our plates, so it was just us, the empty table, and the locket resting between us.

"What's going on?" my dad asked, not making note of how dark the house was, and he opened the fridge. Usually my mom made him a plate when we ate and he peered in and then looked over the door at her. "Dinner?"

I loved my dad. He really wasn't the kind of guy who thought women had to stay home and cook while men worked, even though the question was rude. I knew it was truly a question of surprise, because if there was one thing no one could beat my mother at, it was structure. Everything followed an order and nothing was ever out of place, so when there wasn't a plate of food, the question was innocent even if it was dumb.

"How old is she?" my mom asked.

"Who?"

She picked up the locket and threw it at him. It hit the fridge and bounced off. He watched the slow arc from freezer door to floor, but he didn't reply. Not at first. Then he closed the refrigerator and turned towards us.

"Lily, go to your room," he said.

"She can stay. She should know."

"This isn't about her," my father argued.

"Of course it is. She's your daughter. Don't you want her to know what it's like? Don't you want her to know it will never be good enough? That sooner or later someone will be better? That someone will replace her? How old is she?" she repeated. She was yelling, something she never did. Even when she was mad at me, it was still in a lilt.

"Maureen, it was a mistake. Two weeks. It lasted two weeks."

"Where were you tonight then?"

"I told you. I was at work."

"Why do you still have her locket?" she asked him.

He stood in the dark kitchen, a silhouette of a man I had grown up worshipping, a man who had taught me to play softball and who had helped me study and who was supposed to be the standard by which I judged all future men. I watched him shift back and forth uncomfortably and then he said, "It fell off and I didn't know what to do with it."

"Fell off when?"

"Please don't make me say it," he said. "You know when."

"Where were you?"

"It was in a motel. It was a sleazy motel. Does that make you feel better? That it was as awful as it should have been?" he asked.

"How old is she? Who is she? Where did you find her?"

"She's an intern at work. But I promise... it's over."

"Answer my question," she said. "How old is she?"

"She just finished her freshman year in college. Nineteen, I think."

"You disgust me."

"Maureen, it was stupid, I know. She was-"

"No. I never want to hear about it again. I'm going to bed."

She got up from the table, her tears dried and her entire body free of emotion. She looked at me and spoke. "Lily, remember this. I want you to remember this always. You will never be good enough. Sooner or later, there is always a nineteen-year-old who is better. Anyone you trust will betray you because someone is always better."

"Maureen," my dad pleaded, but my mom pushed in her chair and went upstairs. I was left alone with him in the kitchen. I couldn't see him; the shadows were too thick, but I was glad I couldn't. It became easier to remember him that way as I got older, to remember all men that way. There was a distance between us because no matter how hard you tried, someone was always going to be better than you and loyalty didn't exist. Even my father was a disappointment.

27.

Ten days before my birthday – and almost exactly two months since college started – I'm sitting in Jack's room, reading, while he plays video games. To be fair, he's playing for a class and he has to take notes and write a paper about the experience. Besides, I suppose reading is my entertainment, so neither of us can complain exactly about the workload.

"Do you have a highlighter? Mine's dying," I tell him.

"In the drawer. Top one," he says without looking away from the seven-headed green eagle-cow monster he's being incinerated by on the TV.

I stick my finger between the pages and reach into his dresser for a highlighter. Looking over, I try to find the highlighter, but the drawer is full – with handcuffs, a blindfold, and other things I've mostly only heard about in my travels. I've never seen them in person, that's for sure. "Uh..."

Jack pauses the game and turns around. "Shit. I meant top drawer of the desk."

"Okay," I say and I close the drawer, not sure if we're going to talk about these things and definitely not sure it's my business. I get the highlighter out of the desk and open my book to start reading again. Jack can fill me in if he chooses.

"It's a long story," he says. "Well, I guess it's not that long. But it's a complicated story."

"We're not dating," I remind him. "This is nothing like that. You're my friend. I don't need to know about what you do in your private time."

"It's not that, Lily. Please look at me."

"Jack, it is seriously none of my business. It just took me aback."

He sits beside me. "Look, I've said before that Alana's story is hers to tell, and it is, but she's had it bad, too. When we met, everyone was already saying terrible things about her."

"Things like what?"

"She slept with teachers. There were naked pictures of her on the internet. She would suck your dick for ten bucks. But she wasn't like that, okay? She wasn't. She was the only person in that shit school who didn't judge me and she was my best friend. When we started dating, she was confused. Things had happened in her life. She can tell you if she chooses. But we were both in need of someone. Of course, we were also both young. There were temptations and we were curious. It was something that grew between us naturally, but she was the only girl I'd ever been with and I was the only guy she trusted."

"So she *is* your girlfriend?" I ask. It doesn't matter, but I don't want to make things weird between them.

"No. She was. But life isn't that easy. There's still... we aren't good together. She needs someone stronger than me and I can't stand who I am with her. It isn't her fault. Please understand that. But some relationships are stronger when they have a foundation based on friendship. For us, though, the foundation is already weak for several reasons and we can't be more than we are."

"You still sleep with her, though, right?" I ask.

"I do. *We* do. For years, we've hung on to that part of our relationship. I love her, Lily. I just don't love her in the right way. Physically, though, I'm an idiot."

"I've only been with one guy. I don't really know much about all that," I admit, "but I kind of know what you mean. There's a big difference between what happens on a physical level and then everything else."

"Alana likes to… experiment. She needs something, I don't know, something more. For a list of reasons that she would probably not want me sharing. But I'm not that kind of guy. I don't normally expect that. I mean, God… I just don't want you to think I'm an asshole."

"I'm not a virgin, Jack. I don't care that you like sex. You don't need to protect me just because my experiences have been a lot less interesting in that area."

I don't want to say it, but with the drawer still slightly open and him this close, I'm tempted to ask him to show me. I have no interest in dating him. I don't want to get back into a relationship. My birthday is still coming up and I'm supposed to call Derek or something, although I've kind of been letting that whole thing die, but I know exactly what Jack is talking about. All of the logic doesn't stop the fact that he's really close and he's got nice eyes and his hands are soft and I wouldn't mind seeing if it felt different with someone else. I just don't want to damage this.

"Maybe you and Alana should meet. At least beyond that awkward moment," he says. "I've told her about you."

"You have? What did you tell her?"

"Nothing really. Just that we talked and I've been spending time with you. That we're friends."

He reaches over and closes the drawer. His arm brushes across my knees and I can't deny the attraction, but I need more than that. I don't want a boyfriend. I like being Jack's friend. But when he leans back and his arm crosses a second time, I can't stop from exhaling loudly.

"What's wrong?" he asks.

What's wrong is that I was with the same guy – the only guy I thought I was attracted to – for almost a year and he never made me feel the way you just did. What's wrong is that the last thing I need is a relationship, but if you're already having a physical "friendship" with

Alana, I can't help but think of suggesting it for us. What's wrong is that I want to kiss you and I don't want to want to kiss you. I want to have a friend and not feel like this with you, because it complicates things and I don't need that.

"Nothing," I reply. I desperately need to get out of here, to talk to Kristen, to call Abby, to find someone to tell me what to do. The problem is that Kristen's with Lyle and Abby's in Europe and we only talk over the internet. Even if she could Skype, I am certainly not going to discuss my fantasies online while she's sitting in some internet café in a random European city. I'm already confused about how I feel; I really don't need Jacques or Pierre or some other French-sounding guy to be privy to it.

"Are you sure?"

"I think so. I didn't realize how late it was. I should get going."

He moves away from me and nods. I know he thinks I'm upset, that I think there's something wrong with him, but the problem is that there's something wrong with me.

"I want to meet Alana," I say. "This weekend? Let's do something this weekend, okay? I just need to finish this chapter and I'm sort of tired and I'll probably just finish it in bed and go to sleep."

Jack looks wary, but he agrees.

I can't get out of there fast enough and I'm glad Kristen isn't home when I get in, because I need to lie in the darkness and make sense of what I feel throughout my body. I've never enjoyed sex, but I enjoyed making Derek happy. Something about Jack, though, is changing everything.

28.

When you imagine the world working out the way you hope, you set up these unrealistic expectations for yourself, inevitably leading to disappointment. Throughout high school, I had watched Abby date and I'd heard stories about Derek and other kids in my classes and I'd never even kissed someone. During freshman year, Jake Johnson asked me to the winter semiformal and I went, but after one slow dance, he got bored with me and I ended up spending the night reading a book on the bleachers.

As the years passed, I made Derek into this person in my head who was going to solve everything. If only he would recognize me as something more than his friend's sister... if only he would love me, everything would be perfect. So when I returned to school after my birthday weekend and everything had changed – I wasn't a virgin and Derek was my boyfriend – I don't know what I imagined would happen, but I expected someone to notice. I expected other people to sense the difference. I expected things to be somehow new, but not in the way that they were.

I told Abby first in study hall.

"You know how I've always said I wouldn't date?" I asked her.

"Yeah, unless Derek comes to his senses, you're going to be celibate forever. I know."

"I wanted to text you, but you were at the wedding and then... well, I spent the last two days with him while he was home and I didn't want to tell you over the phone."

"Tell me what?" she asked and then she began to understand. "Shit. Don't even tell me. You didn't."

"Yeah."

"Was it amazing? Was it everything you'd thought it be for years?"

It wasn't, of course, but I didn't want her to know that. I didn't want to tell her, because I was afraid it was me. I was afraid Derek would get back to school and wonder what he'd been thinking and I believed if I pretended everything was as amazing as I had built it up to be that it would actually evolve into that.

"It was."

"I can't believe you waited until now to tell me. Aunt Ethel's corns really could have waited."

"Is that what you did all weekend?"

She laughed. "Seriously, Lily." She went on to tell me about the wedding, although I struggled to listen. My life was different now, but I guess by senior year of high school, it was no longer interesting to my best friend that I'd had sex. I didn't think it was interesting to anyone, since most people had – or at least said they had – and I wasn't unique or even the kind of person anyone noticed.

That should have been it. A confession to a friend in study hall that didn't affect anyone beyond her, me, and Derek. If he was telling anyone, it was at school and I sincerely doubted college kids cared that he'd had sex over the weekend. From what he and Jon had said, it sounded like that was a lot of what happened in college.

I barely knew Miranda Elliot. She was popular, I guess, but we didn't have classes together and none of my friends talked to hers. Abby was the only person I was close to, but my small group of acquaintances from track and Student Council and my lunch table were just not the same kinds of people Miranda Elliot hung around with. She wasn't some stereotypical mean girl like in a bad movie; she was just a girl who played soccer and lived in another neighborhood.

So I certainly didn't expect her to come stand over me while I was eating lunch. And I really didn't expect her to lean down and demean my relationship. Her breath was against my ear as she said it. "I fucked him, too. You're nothing special."

"What are you talking about?" I asked.

"Everyone knows. Lacey heard you and Abby talking in study hall. You feel like you're somehow special, right, because you fucked Derek LaGrange? You know that almost everyone here has fucked him, right?"

"It's none of your business."

"It's my business when some slut goes around bragging because she's the only girl Derek loves."

"Shut up, Miranda," Abby said, but she wasn't the target. She wasn't the slut, as Miranda referred to me, although she had been with him, too. I sat there while they argued, while they insulted one another, and I sat

there listening to Miranda talk about Derek and the weekends she'd spent hooking up with him over the summer. I had to listen to all the things he had told her, and I tried not to hear them, because they were the same things he had told me. I knew about him and all the other girls and I knew what I was getting into, but I still thought I was different. None of them had known him before. None of them knew him when they were kids and he was a dorky guy with braces. None of them had waited and saved every part of themselves for him.

"It's not the same thing," I whispered finally, but my voice was like tissue paper against a hurricane. Although I was shaking, I hated conflict and I just wanted her to go away. I wanted her to take her experiences and her memories of Derek and her cries of slut and I just wanted her to disappear. I didn't want to argue or to change her mind, as long as she just left me alone.

"Really, Lily? How is it different? Do you really think he loves you?" Miranda asked.

"He does. He told me he loves me," I said, and it was stupid. Abby shook her head, but she still thought that *maybe Derek and I had a chance. It had only been a few days and at first, she believed it, too.*

"He says that to everyone, you know. But enjoy. I was a virgin before Derek, too. I think that's his favorite kind."

Sex was supposed to be special. It was supposed to be at least pleasant. It wasn't supposed to be the biggest story in my high school within days of it happening, especially when no one had noticed me at all for the first three years. It didn't make sense that anyone cared about it except me, even though I'd been disappointed when they hadn't noticed. I didn't know much about it, really, but I knew it wasn't supposed to make me feel guilty, and I knew I wasn't supposed to call Derek to talk about it only to be told to stop acting like a child.

"Everyone does it, Lily. It's just sex."

None of these things were what happened in my imagined relationship with Derek, but as memories slowly drain themselves into my present, I wonder how I survived imagining for so long.

29.

Alana is the most intimidating person I've ever met. She's beautiful and honest and she looks at me like she can read every secret, but she doesn't want to rush to judge. I don't know how to understand a person who doesn't judge, who looks at you fully and tries to see the whole picture.

I don't know where Jack went. I came over and he was here and Alana was here and now he's gone. I don't know how to talk to her.

"I think you scare me," she says.

"Why?"

"I'm pretty sure Jack has never met anyone like you. He usually goes for people as fucked up as he is and he doesn't do relationships. But he talks about you a lot."

"We're just friends," I say. "I have – or had – a boyfriend. I don't really need to think about that right now."

"He's a good guy. Don't hurt him."

"I wasn't planning on it. We're just friends."

"There's no such thing," she argues. "He and I tried just friends. Then we tried something serious. And now, well, I don't know anymore. But for a while we had everything."

"Are you in love with him?" I ask.

"Yes, but not in the way you're asking."

"I don't know any other way."

So far, college hasn't been much different than high school, as far as the people. My classes are mostly made up of other freshman and the only people I really know, besides Jack, are freshman or I don't talk to them past a superficial level. But Alana is less than two years older than me – and I feel like she's from a distant planet. I always viewed Abby as contrary, because she had opinions and wasn't afraid of them, but Alana is the kind of girl I admire. In quiet, because I'm too scared to live the way she does.

"Guys like to fuck me," she tries to explain. When she says it, it doesn't sound crass, at least not in the way one would expect. She says it the same way she would give directions. "Always have. I don't think I bring a lot to the table, you know, otherwise. But with Jack... the thing is, when he fucks you, he makes you feel like you are the only girl in the world."

"I'm not sleeping with him. It's not like that," I repeat.

"Has he told you about us?"

"Not exactly. He said it's mostly your story to tell. I mean, I saw the things in the drawer-"

She laughs. "Look. I like you. It makes me nervous how much Jack likes you, because you're too much of an anomaly. If you were some kind of conquest for him, I could understand it. If you were a challenge, maybe, but I don't know what you are."

"That makes two of us."

"We're not still a thing," she tells me. "If that's your hang up. We haven't... not since that day you walked in. What was it – a few weeks ago?"

"Almost. But it's not that long. I mean, people don't change that fast. Feelings don't change that fast."

"No, they don't. But the feelings aren't what you think they are. Has he told you about all of us? Me and Dave and him? How things went?"

"Not really."

"Do you want the short or the shorter version?" she asks.

"It doesn't matter. I'm just curious."

She takes off her coat and hands it to me without explanation and then lifts off her long-sleeved black shirt. Wearing only her bra, she holds out her arms. The skin is pale, making the scar tissue – both ghostly white and an angry red – stand out more against her flesh. Each arm, from wrist to elbow, is a patchwork of lines.

"I lost my virginity at eleven. To my dad. I thought it was a fluke, until my mom remarried and my stepdad did the same and worse. They made me ugly, but only on the inside, and I needed to remind myself how ugly I really was. I needed men to see what they made me."

"I'm sorry," I say.

"You didn't do it."

"I know. But God. I don't know what to say. I've been so concerned about my problems, when you and Jack have lived through things I never would have survived."

Alana puts her shirt back on. "That's dumb. We all have problems. That's the point. I have problems. Jack has problems. And our friend, Dave, who's gone now, he had problems, too. But they were the only two guys who could see the scars and face them. Out there are people who have it worse than any of the three of us do, but the point is that once you can see yourself through the eyes of someone who thinks even your scars are beautiful, the things that matter change."

"And that's your relationship?" I ask.

"It is. It *was*. We're bad for each other. We have been through so much damage, both together and apart, that it's hard to disassociate that with the person. I love him, but it's just not the way it should be. And then there's Dave."

"Did you date him?"

She sighs. "I fell for Jack right away," she confesses. "Immediately. The first time I saw him, I knew. He had no friends and when I talked to him in our math class, we just clicked, you know? I was a loser, too, and everyone made up stories about me. But he didn't see that. He just talked to me and even though we were both nothing, together we were something special. All of the places in me that were empty fit with all the places he wasn't. I felt like I'd found the only friend I'd ever need."

"But?"

"But we were fourteen. And the things that happened with my stepdad happened before I could be okay, and it was always a part of me and Jack. It's a long story and it's not one I want to go into, but we can say that we never had a chance. And then we met Dave and I cared for him and he cared for me, but Jack was first. It's not always that simple, of course, and we fought about it, but then high school ended and Dave went to the Army and he said it was best if he just let us go. I've spent three years missing him. I recently got back in touch, but it's all kinds of complicated, and basically, it just leaves a big mess. But Jack and I are both ready to accept what we are for each other and try to let it go. I'll never live a life without him, but I'm not going to be in your way."

"There's no way," I argue.

"There might be. Someday. And given Jack's history-"

She's about to continue when Jack comes back. He's carrying a bag of food and I watch him while he unpacks it. I've been so wrapped up in myself that all I've noticed really were his eyes. He carries so much emotional weight on him and it affects the way he moves, like every memory is pushing him down. It hurts to look at him, because I see so much kindness in him but now I can also see his pain. When he smiles at me, though, he's hard to look away from – and I know what Alana means about seeing the beauty in a person's scars.

"What did you talk about?" he asks. He brought Chinese food and my stomach growls when I see it, but then I feel like throwing up. It's greasy when he scoops it onto a plate and I take it, grateful, but I know I won't be able to eat it.

"Oh, you know," Alana says. "Stuff."

She takes a bite of her chicken. I can smell it, both the sauce and the grease, and I need to vomit. I need to get out of this warm room where people have it worse than I do and can still be okay. I need to run back to my room and hide and lose myself in memories again, a place where I didn't see things for what they were.

30.

When we were little, my brother was my best friend. This all came before Derek, before Abby, before my mom began to hold us to different standards.

All summer, we lived in our own imagined world. The woods were our kingdom, and the stumps of old trees our castle. We were supposed to come inside when it got dark and we usually did. We loved the woods, but they were still scary for us at that age and at night, we believed the monsters came out.

Earlier in the day, my father had bought us plastic swords from Wal-Mart during his morning errands and Jon and I were fighting a battle with a massive troll. The troll was a gnarled tree, with moss that crawled along its trunk, and the roots were digging their way upwards out of the dirt.

"Give me your sister, so she can be my troll queen," Jon said in his best troll voice.

"Never," he replied as himself. He brandished his sword and swung at the mossy bark. A caterpillar went sailing into the forest behind us. "Lily is the princess and I will protect her."

My ankle was itchy from cutting it on a briar on our way into the woods and I hopped back and forth, trying to balance on one foot while scratching it with my sword. "You won't take me alive," I taunted the troll tree.

"Very well," said troll-Jon. "I will send my minions to capture you and then cook you in a stew. You could have been a queen."

"Why are my choices troll queen or stew?" I asked.

Jon broke character for a moment. "Because that's how villains are, Lily. You do what they say or they send out minions."

"It seems dumb. I think he should try to convince me. I mean, all he did was tell you to give me to him. Shouldn't he negotiate?"

"What's negotiate?" Jon asked.

"I don't know. Dad told Mom he had to negotiate so they would give him more money at work if she wanted to go on vacation next week."

"I'll ask." Pulling down his Halloween costume helmet, Jon approached the tree again. "Your evilness, the Troll King. We would like to negotiate."

"I see. I suppose we can do that," the troll agreed.

Jon turned around and lifted his helmet again, whisper-shouting, "Now what?"

"I don't know. I don't know what it means. Maybe it's like a bargain?"

"I'll ask," he said again and returned to the troll.

"We would like to bargain with you for Lily as your queen."

"I have already declared her a stew," troll-Jon replied. "And you swore to protect her."

"That is my bargain. My sister, Lily, will be your queen, but you must keep her safe. And you must allow me to live in the same castle and make sure."

"Also I want a puppy," I said. "And cookies." I decided if I was going to be forced to marry a tree troll, the least I could do was demand something for myself.

Jon leaned close to the tree, as if he and the troll were whispering and discussing the bargain. He turned around and faced me, his helmet still up.

"The troll cannot give you a puppy because he is stuck in the mud. But he says he'll send his minions to force Mom to bake cookies for your wedding and it will be a cookie feast."

I scratched my ankle again. "What about you?"

"He has agreed that I can live in the castle, too, and eat the cookies. He also promises to keep you safe from the ogres who come out at night."

"That works."

I easily resigned myself to my fate as the troll queen and Jon ran into the house to grab a box of Oreos, which were the closest thing we had to homemade cookies. I ate them and fed one into the hole inside the tree's trunk, pretending it was like at weddings when couples shove cake in each other's faces. Jon made me a garland for my head from some branches he found, but one had a spider on it and it fell into the Oreos.

"Ew, spiders," I said, the Oreos now upside down in the dirt.

"You're married to a troll, Lily. You can't be afraid of spiders," Jon argued.

"I can be afraid of whatever I want. You're not doing a very good job protecting me. I think maybe I'll turn you into a stew after all."

"You can't turn me into a stew. I saved you."

We played that afternoon, pretending it was my troll wedding, and threatening to have each other turned into a stew. Eventually I got bored being a queen and had Jon help me assassinate the troll, because I wanted power, not to sit around and feed a tree cookies.

As it started to get dark, we picked up our Oreo bag and swords. "I'm going to have to fight the ogres now," I told Jon. "One day, they're going to come out before we get home and I killed the troll."

"Well, if they dare to come after you, I'll stop them. No one is going to hurt my sister," he said. "I'll always protect you, Lily, from ogres and trolls and anything else that comes out at night."

"And spiders?"

"And spiders. That's my job as your big brother."

When Jon and I got older and it wasn't normal anymore for us to play in the woods and fight trees we envisioned as trolls, I think I still imagined that the rest of it was true. That big brothers really did protect their sisters – from ogres and spiders and anything else that scared them. But sometimes imagination isn't just about turning a tree into something scary. Sometimes, I guess, it's about seeing something real as better than it is.

31.

What's funny about believing a lie you tell yourself is that it's easy to forget you ever believed it in the first place. When you don't use all that energy building up a façade, you find you have a lot more time to focus on what's real. Spending time with Jack and being at school has been buffering the memories and I've gotten used to the idea that this is the only life I've led. When I went home for Columbus Day, I felt like school was some sort of vacation, but now home feels distant, like it's a movie I've seen too many times.

I finally finished my paper on Marianne and although I don't know that it was an improvement, at least I did something different. Lit Study has moved on to *Tess of the d'Urbervilles* and I'm pondering her complicated beginnings on my walk back to the dorm. I think nothing of the voices coming from my room until I get closer. Kristen is talking to a guy, but I expect it to be Lyle or maybe Don. I definitely don't expect it to be Derek.

"What are you doing here?" I ask. "You weren't supposed to come up for a couple weeks."

"I thought we should talk," he says.

"Oh, okay." I don't know what to do or how to react. He shouldn't feel like a stranger, but suddenly, Derek being here, in my room, feels invasive. Kristen looks at us both and excuses herself. I can't imagine what she must be thinking.

As soon as she's gone, Derek is all over me. His hands are in my shirt, his mouth is near mine, and he's saying things, but I just want him to stop.

"Stop," I tell him.

"Why?"

"Just stop." I move away from him and sit on my bed. The heater is going, but it's freezing in here. He sits beside me after taking off his shirt and he reaches for my belt loops, kissing my neck and telling me how much he's missed me.

"You broke up with me," I say, trying to move away from him.

"Lily, I've been an ass, come on. Let me make it up to you."

"I need you to stop touching me," I tell him, pushing his hands away. "Please, Derek. I don't want to."

"You're ridiculous. I'm trying to fix it. Stop fighting me."

"I don't want to have sex with you."

I want to run out of the room, to get Kristen or someone to help, but I don't. He's still Derek. He's still friends with my brother. Sure, he's not listening, but I'm not scared of him. Not until he pushes me hard against the wall.

"I gave up a lot to date you, you know," he says. "I broke things off with Jodie. I've been faithful to you, even when it wasn't easy, even when you were a pain in the ass. I miss you when I'm at school. I'm sorry I made you feel bad, but it's been forever, Lily. I need you. I need this. Stop acting like you don't want it. You've never said no before."

"I don't want it," I reply. "At all. Get away from me."

He doesn't. I can't fight him and I'm on my back and he's on me and I don't understand. It's not even the fact that he's undressing me, that I'm nearly naked and so is he and that he's planning to do this, despite that fact that I said no. What scares me more than anything is that the boy I fell in love with, the boy in the tent who made me want to have a boyfriend and to be pretty, was always the kind of person who would do this. People don't *become* this kind of person; they just are or they aren't. How did I not see this?

"Please don't," I beg. He's not gentle and I'm in my underwear and bra and his hands are between my legs and I can't stop him. I can't, because I never said no and he thinks this is okay. I can't even scream, because I don't know how to make sense of any of it. "Please, Derek."

I wish I knew what changed his mind. I wish I could express it and capture it and use it if this ever happened again, but I don't. He was pushing all his weight down on me, his fingers exploring, and I was sure that my boyfriend or ex-boyfriend or whatever he is was going to rape me, but then he stopped. In a moment, he stopped and now he's staring at me, the anger still seething, but his hands are by his side again and I can move.

"You should go," I say.

"Lily, I miss you. Don't be like this. I'm sorry. You do this to me, though. You're just so sexy and I can't help myself. Please don't make me beg. I need it. Please."

"I don't think so. I think you need to go." The room feels like ice now, but I don't think it has anything to do with the heat.

"Are you cheating on me?" he snaps. "Is that why?"

"We broke up," I remind him.

"So that makes it okay for you to be a slut as soon as I need a break. I had schoolwork. I told you it wasn't about us, that I needed time to get my grades up and to focus on rugby. I didn't tell you to come back here and just be a whore."

"I haven't touched anyone," I say. "I'm far from being a slut. You can't be serious, with all the girls you've slept with. You probably *did* cheat on me."

"Nothing serious."

"So you did?"

"No, not really. I mean, there were a few nights I was drunk and Jodie and I had already slept together before you, and you weren't around, but it didn't mean anything. I still love you. It wasn't cheating, because it wasn't new."

"You really need to go," I tell him again.

He doesn't move and I want to hurt him. I want to make him feel everything I've felt for a year, everything I convinced myself was normal just because I wanted us to be okay. Just because I believed in a boy who listened and who cared about adventures and who seemed like he could love me. Maybe I don't warrant real love, but I realize I definitely deserve better than this.

I wish the knock on the door wasn't real. I wish I could cry out and stop it. I wish a lot of things, but wishing doesn't stop Derek from opening the door. Jack looks confused and a little nervous. I can't meet his eyes, shame breaking me into a million tiny pieces. Derek's standing there with his shirt off and his pants undone and I'm clinging to my clothes because I was afraid to get dressed, to set him off, to do anything, and now Jack is seeing this and I can't explain. We aren't in a relationship and I owe him nothing, but I still want him to know that this isn't me.

Derek pushes Jack back so he hits the wall across the hallway. "Who the fuck are you? Are you the guy who ruined her?"

Jack doesn't fight back. Not at first. He just stares across the hall at Derek and I rush to get my clothes on. "I'm certainly not the guy who calls her ruined," Jack says, which pisses Derek off more and he grabs Jack by the throat. I see it in Jack's eyes – the doubt that he's a bad person, the internal debate about fighting back, and his recognition of the tears I can't stop now – and he snaps. He twists out of Derek's grip and swings at him. The punch connects with Derek's jaw, which just makes it a million times worse. Derek hits Jack and it knocks him to the ground, but Jack is all rage now.

"Stop. Both of you. Derek, you need to leave. Now."

"Fuck you, bitch," he says, but he grabs his shirt and takes off, leaving me and Jack in the hall, both of us shaking and he turns me towards my room and leads me inside.

"Are you okay?"

"I'm fine," I say, but I can't look at him. I don't want him to see me like this.

"Do you want me to leave?" he asks from the doorway.

"I don't know. Yeah, probably." It's not his fault and I don't want to blame him, but I need to be alone. I don't want to touch anyone or talk to anyone or even try to explain what just happened. I don't want to think about it or to have it be true. I just want to curl up and go to sleep and tell myself that it was a bad dream. All of this is a bad dream.

"I'm going to stay in my room," Jack says. "I'll text you every hour. You don't have to answer. But if you need me, I'll set my alarm on my phone. Every hour, Lily. And when you're ready or if you can't sleep or if you need to walk in circles, you can reply. If I fall asleep, it will only be an hour, okay?"

I nod, but I can't talk to him. He leaves and I close the door and grab a sweatshirt from my closet. Even under the blankets and with the sweatshirt, I can't stop shaking. I want to remember something else, anything else, but my mind can't remember. All that exists is right now.

32.

It's hard to remember anything when you know you've lied to yourself for your entire life.

PART III:

Flying

33.

"Can I talk to Alana?" I ask Jack. He's done as he promised and checked on me every hour for three days now. I haven't even told Kristen what happened. I was asleep when she came back the night Derek was here and then I just told her that we broke up for good.

"Sure. I mean, yeah. I'll have her call you. Are you okay?" I've only texted him since that night and it feels good to hear his voice, but I'm not ready to talk to him about it yet.

"I will be. I think."

"I'll call her right now, okay?"

She texts me quick, but since she didn't go away to school, she can't visit for a couple hours and I don't want to talk over the phone. So I pace and I think about eating. I could get fat. No one would care. Well, my mother would but somehow she feels complicit in all of this.

Kristen watches me while I wait for Alana, but she says nothing. I feel guilty. She was my friend when I had none. I should tell her. I should text Abby and talk to her somehow, but there's never privacy talking to her and right now, Europe might as well be Jupiter.

The first thing I do when Alana and I get to the café is tell her about Prom. I tell her how Derek was, how he made fun of everyone and how he told me a hundred times the night was stupid. I tell her about after, in the hotel he'd argued with me about renting before finally saying he would only go if I did. I tell her how he told me about things other girls did and how he said I would do them, too, if I really loved him. I tell her all about how stupid and naïve and worthless and broken I felt, but how after, I believed him and I tried to forget, because he said he cared and he told me I was perfect. Then I tell her about the last year, about Jodie, about the girls who came before, about camping, and I tell her about how it's been. I tell her about the breakup and then, finally, I tell her what happened the other night.

"Did he rape you?" she asks.

"No. That's just it. He stopped before it went that far, but he was mean and I thought he was going to. I know I don't have a right to feel like this. So what? My boyfriend pressures me to have sex and then gets mad when, after a year, I suddenly don't want to? That's not a crime and it's not worth feeling like this over."

She pushes the coffee she ordered for me towards me, but I don't want it. I don't want anything. It's too hot and when I sip at it, I can feel the heat sliding down my body in my veins. It makes me feel present, reminds me of how flawed every inch of me is, and I get nauseous remembering how he pushed me.

"No one ever has the right to make you feel like you do. How you want to define it is up to you and what you want to do next is also your choice, but he's gone. He can't decide for you, Lily."

"I just feel wrong about feeling this way. What about you? You told me horrible things and here I am, whining about nothing."

"It's not a contest. It's not about who's more fucked up. There are no levels of feeling like shit. There's just being okay – and not being okay. And you're not okay. So how do we fix that?"

I look out the window at the parking lot. Stray carriages are rolling across the lot, pushed by invisible people with invisible lives. I wonder if they can see me or if I'm just an invisible girl, too. "Does it bother you that I asked you?" I ask Alana. "I mean, that I could only talk to you about it?"

"We're a secret club that no one wants to be a member of," she replies. "The girls men use. But it sounds so awful to say it. I don't hate men. I don't hate sex. I just hate that I feel like I hear this story every day."

"Can I ask you something?"

She drinks her coffee and gets up to refill it without answering. When she comes back, I notice how tired she looks. She's only 20, but she's exhausted by living. "Ask away. I'm ready."

"How do you trust anyone? Why do you trust Jack? What happened with him? How can you enjoy sex? And the things in his room... doesn't that...?" I don't finish, because that's more than one something and she's smiling, but I can see she asks herself the same questions all the time.

"That's a lot of things to explain. I don't trust people, not really, but I try to rationalize some of it. I spend a lot of time in therapy and I take too many pills to numb what I really feel and think. I don't know why I enjoy sex, because the physical act does one thing but it still bothers me when I'm alone. I talk to my therapist about that, too. As far as the kind of sex I like and have, well, you can't change your body or your physical responses any more than you can change who you are or how you feel. Just because those guys were the way they were doesn't mean they get to decide how I'm going to find my own satisfaction. It's not a question of that, really. It's a question of reconciling it and justifying it for myself and that's what I'm working on. You know. In all the therapy."

"Should I be angry?" I ask.

"*Are* you angry?"

"I think so. It's hard to piece it together. All my memories of him, of my mom, of my life – they all made sense and nothing seemed odd about them. But in the last few days, I haven't slept well. They all keep coming back to me, but I'm seeing them new. I'm seeing them like someone who didn't live them and I want to tell that girl what kind of person he is, to tell her she isn't the reason her mom is so angry, that she has every right to want someone to listen. But when I realize that girl is me, I can't believe those things."

"Why?" Alana asks. "What's so bad about you?"

"I don't know," I admit. "I just don't think it's as easy as all that."

She finishes her second coffee and looks at mine. The cream has formed a layer over the top and I can't look at it. I wish I knew why everything made me feel so empty.

"You should eat something. Drink something. I know it's hard. I know everyone will have advice and nothing will make sense, but trust me, the worst place you can be right now is alone in your head."

I can't drink the coffee, so I bring it back to the barista, but I force myself to buy – and drink – a small carton of orange juice. It's something.

We take our time walking back to campus, because I'm still trying to put all of these pieces of myself together. A girl who was never good enough. A girl who is trying to start new. And now the girl who never speaks up but is tired of silence.

"Are you still in love with him? Like in the way you were?" I ask Alana.

"No, I don't think so. We were kids. I loved him because he made me stronger, but that's not the same as being in love with someone. At sixteen, I thought it was, and that's just hard to shake."

"Yeah."

"With Jack, it's need. Physical need. Something in each of us is broken. We cling to each other like it will hold us together. It's hard," she continues, "when someone is so important to you, to let go, to see it for what it is. But neither of us has a claim to the other."

"I'm not ready, not for him," I admit to her. "I'm not ready for someone to care like he does."

"Don't close him out, Lily. He's a good guy. He deserves to believe in something, too."

34.

It's been a week and I haven't been leaving my room much. Most days I sleep until midday and then stare at the TV. I try to read, but it's hard to care much about Tess' problems. I have enough of my own. Kristen, Jack, and Lyle alternate, coming in to invite me to go to lunch or dinner, listening to my excuses, and then showing up with a meal in Styrofoam because "there was extra." The college meal policy is really strict about taking food from the cafeteria, because for half a million dollars or whatever it costs a year, we certainly can't go over our meal plan.

I need to go to my classes. We just finished midterms and I'm doing well, but I can't afford to miss class. Despite knowing that, though, I can't get out of bed. Everything about me feels wrong. I know Alana said it wasn't wrong and that I had a right to feel this way, but I don't. And it's just another thing about me that's not good enough.

My parents keep calling. We haven't talked since Columbus Day, but they left messages on my birthday and I didn't call back, and now there's Thanksgiving. My mom will want to know what I'm going to wear. I don't want to talk to them. I don't want to go home. I'll have to hear about Derek and I'll have to pretend it doesn't hurt and I'll have to stop remembering what he's really like. At the same time, I do want to go home, though, because Abby is flying back until after Christmas and I need her desperately.

"I brought you a sandwich and some cookies. I couldn't smuggle anything else out," Kristen says on her way into the room. She reaches into her purse and pulls out bologna and cheese on a bulky and two sugar cookies, all wrapped in a pile of napkins.

"Thanks. I'm not hungry, but thank you for making your purse smell like lunchmeat for me."

She laughs. "You should eat, though. I won't tell you to talk to me about whatever happened, but you should eat."

"I can't. The smell of the sandwich is making me sick," I admit.

"Well, great, because you get to live with it until I can wash my bag."

"How's Lyle?" I ask.

"He's all right. He's doing something tonight. I don't know. The environmental club. You were in that, weren't you?"

"I think I still am. Not that I've been going to things. I'm going to be fired from the paper," I realize aloud.

"I wouldn't worry about it. The post-modern ska/bluegrass infusion band can probably wait two weeks for your review."

Living with another person is strange, especially if you never have before. She drops her bag on the chair, pulls her sweater over her head, and steps out of her jeans, looking for something to relax in wearing only her bra and underwear. She's comfortable and it's odd that a few months ago, we didn't even know each other's last names. Once she finds clothes, she jumps up onto her bed and throws a bottle of water at me from the crate next to her.

"You're missing the fall," she says.

223

"I hate the fall."

"Still, there are pumpkins and leaves and it's cold, but not freezing yet. Good cider weather. You missed Halloween."

I did miss Halloween, the holiday that I always want to be exciting but ends up disappointing me. This year, I slept through it. "And my birthday," I tell her.

"I know."

"Does it matter? Nineteen isn't different than eighteen. It's never different, is it?"

Kristen looks around the room, at the pile of clothes I need to wash, at my books for classes piled up and dog-eared but starting to collect dust, at the bologna sandwich she'll end up cleaning up because I'll just let it sit there.

"My chemistry class sucks."

"Why are you even taking that?" I ask.

"I don't know. They want me to be well-rounded. I guess I can't effectively teach children about vowels without understanding noble gases."

"Clearly."

"It's a lot of work, and I don't really see the point. But I guess you have to do it, right?"

"I was good at chemistry," I reply. "In high school, I mean. Although it's probably harder in college."

She reaches into her backpack, which is shoved into a corner at one end of the bed, and takes out her chemistry book. "I think this is the same book my high school used," she says. "It's science for elementary ed majors. They assume we're stupid."

"Says a lot about their hope for future generations of educated youth."

"No kidding. Anyway, I have to write a paper about valence electrons or something. Does that mean anything to you?"

I move over to her bed and we spend the next few hours on valence electrons, atomic structure, and chemical reactions. It's the first time since school started that I feel like I'm *at* school, that this is the actual point of college. My days and nights are full of experiences, but I'm only in classes a few hours a week. And lately, no hours a week.

"That makes a lot of sense," Kristen says, "although I still don't think I'll ever really need this."

"Maybe not, but at least now you get it."

"What about your classes?" she asks. "How are they? Have you talked to anyone? I mean, to explain missing them?"

I shake my head. "Not really. I mean, I haven't missed any actual work exactly, but I have a ton of reading to catch up on and some of my professors aren't all that flexible about attendance policies."

"Just talk to them. I'm sure there is something you can do."

"I should probably at least finish the books first, right?"

"It's Wednesday. Go back Monday? That'll give you time to catch up?"

Jumping off her bed, I nod. "Yeah. I guess I can do that."

She packs up her book and notes and turns on her laptop to check email. Since I need to pee, I head out into the hall for the bathroom. I can't help but look, because I do it every time I leave the room, but Jack isn't conveniently turning a corner from the other wing. I should go to talk to him, to say more than a few syllables when he shows up with food, but if reading a book is this complicated, I'm not sure I'm much company anyway. *It'll get better*, I tell myself, and though I don't believe it, I try to see it as law. It has to, doesn't it? No one can feel like this all the time.

****

I try to keep the memories out, try to think about nothing but the moment. They keep bringing me food, looking after me, and motivating me to go to classes. I haven't told them the story. It's been tough because we're still reading *Tess of the d'Urbervilles* and I don't want to write about it. I don't want to talk about what happened to me or to her, and I certainly don't want to sit in class and listen to people argue how much of it was her fault. How can they say things like that? Do they really think it or do they just like to be heard? I wonder what it's like to be so desperate to be heard that you lose sight of what you're even saying.

Kristen and Lyle both went home for the weekend, so Jack's on food duty. I'm trying to force myself to write something meaningful about Tess when he knocks. I open the door and find him in the hallway, his hair still wet from the shower. He's wearing a dress shirt and corduroys, which is first time I've seen him out of jeans.

"It's stupid and I know you're still avoiding me, but-"

"I'm not avoiding you," I reply. "I'm just trying to make sense of things."

"I know, and it's fine and you can open this and I'll leave." He hands me a card and a small box he was holding behind his back. "But if you're not busy and you want to hang out tonight, I thought I could take you out. For your birthday."

"That was weeks ago," I say.

"Fifteen days. And it just passed and that's not all right, so..." He stands there in the hall, looking worried, his hands in his pockets. I wanted it to pass unnoticed, but I feel bad telling him I don't appreciate the thought. I *do* appreciate it. I'm just not sure I deserve it.

"Give me an hour," I tell him. "I'll come to your room."

It's not a date, I remind myself after he leaves. I need to decide how to manage this. I don't have many friends, never mind guy friends, never mind guys I find attractive despite how much I tell myself that I can't do this right now. I have no intention of doing this –

whatever *this* may be – but it doesn't mean I can turn off the idea that I want to impress him. Everything I've learned about relationships was with Derek, or through my mom's direction, and I don't know how to be just me. Jack has told me he wants me to be myself with him, but how, when I have no idea who that is?

My birthday feels so meaningless. How can it be important, when less than two weeks ago, I was seeing my life for the first time? It didn't take what happened with Derek – and I still haven't decided what that is or what to call it – for me to realize that I wasn't whole anymore. I hid it and I lied to myself, like I do, but it was true that I'd lost something between home and school. I knew I had been clinging to the past. I knew that I was becoming nothing but a shadow of a person, given that memory was only illusion. To continue to remember means to forgive. I'm no longer capable of forgiving, and I think I like that realization most of all. Some things don't deserve forgiveness.

I end up settling on jeans and a sweater – casual and not indicative of anything – before fixing my hair and heading to Jack's room. He opens the door immediately, as if he's been waiting behind it for the last hour. "Did you open it?" he asks.

In my getting ready, I left his gift and card on my desk and forgot. "I'm sorry. I will when we get back. I was trying to figure out what to wear."

"You look really nice."

"Thanks. So what are these big plans?"

He grabs his jacket and leads me into the hallway. "It's probably stupid, but do you trust me?"

"I do," I reply, before I even know I'm saying it. I *do* trust him, although I've known him for two months, yet he feels like the closest friend I've had in ages. "Wow. Yeah. I do."

"I'm glad."

It's going to snow, but it hasn't yet, which is worse. There is the same painful cold that settles, a warning of the storm to come, but it just waits and aches while the snow builds. My sweater and coat aren't enough to keep off the wind, but I don't want to complain. My parents left a few messages for my birthday and sent me an e-card that I couldn't get to play, but that was the full extent of my celebration. At the bottom of my e-card, my mother added a note that I should try to avoid eating before Thanksgiving if I didn't "want to be a whale by Christmas." I can't help but feel like the wind, therefore, is worth it, just to spend time with someone who actually cares.

When we get to his car, Jack waits, hesitating by the hood. "Do you want me to open your door?" he asks.

"Why?"

"I don't know. I just wanted… I want to be nice. But I don't want you to think that I think you need to have your door opened."

Laughing, I open the door myself and climb into the passenger seat. Jack turns on the heat and we wait for the car to start, music quietly filling the space between us. It's not that late, but the sky is already a blanket of stars. With the trees all dead, it's easy to see the light through the broken parts.

"Tell me about your band," I say and rest my head on the seat. Jack is comfortable. It's easy to spend time with him.

"What about them? We're okay. I mean, I have no plans of doing it past school, but it's good for when things get bad. Sometimes I need a place to drain myself of the darkness."

"Do things still get bad?"

"All the time," he admits. "I'm not easy to know, Lily. In ten minutes, for no reason at all, I could shut down. I don't plan on it, but I could. When I do, there's no way out. There's no escape from it. I live in a constant state of knowing that I'm just one failed kick from drowning."

"Yet you've been there through everything for me."

"I care. I don't know why I care, I'll be honest, but I can't help it."

"I'm happy you're honest," I say. "I'd rather you tell me how things really are. I've spent too long not knowing, being protected and sheltered from what I didn't want to see."

"Are you ready for the full truth?" he asks.

"Of course."

I haven't been watching the road, but we're heading out of town and away from everything I know. A month ago, that would have scared me, but now the thought of a whole road and horizon full of something else is what keeps me from letting the thought of Derek and his hands on me, holding me down, ruin this. I've given him too many years of my life. We're celebrating my birthday, another year, and there isn't going to be space for him in this one.

"I play bass because I can't sing," Jack says. "I used to like singing, but my vocal cords are screwed up now."

"Your voice sounds fine."

He shakes his head and turns off the music. Even though the heat is on full, small wisps of cold reach me through the spaces between the window and the door and another hits me as he starts to speak.

"During my senior year of high school, I tried to die. I stood in my grandmother's bathroom for three hours and I couldn't find a single reason to go on. I tried. Lily, I wanted nothing more than to *want* to be alive, but I couldn't. I thought about leaving a note, thinking I had the words. I believed it was a matter of finding the right ones, of putting them together like a person weaves a blanket. Once I found the pattern and I made my home with the words, my voice would finally be more than a silent echo. Is that ironic? Oxymoronic? Is it possible to have a silent echo?"

"I don't know, but I'm glad you didn't die," I tell him. I imagine this semester, the night with Derek, sitting here now, and how none of this would have existed. *He* wouldn't have existed. How can it hurt so badly to imagine losing something you didn't even know you needed?

"Thanks, but the problem was that after three hours, the words didn't come. Inside the mirror, I saw myself, but I was surrounded by nothing but hopelessness. I wanted to scream, but I knew the only thing that would come back would be desperation. Being alive was a burden and I didn't want to face it anymore."

He stops speaking and pulls the car to the side of the road. His hands are shaking and he's staring at the road and tree line, although I know he can only see the blackness that was reflected in that mirror years ago.

"Tell me," I say, reaching out a hand and resting it on his forearm. It's not a big move although it terrifies me. I can't stop thinking about that night and what it felt like to hear those words, to be touched that way and called a slut and a whore. I know it wasn't Jack, but the sweeping nausea still seeps into my veins. But I don't let go of his arm, because I want to care despite it all.

He turns to face me and his blue eyes are blazing with pain. "I don't have the words, Lily. I can't explain how it felt, how helpless but at the same time so sure. It was like one of those old fun houses, where the mirrors only reflect distortions, the world as you've imagined it be. I watched the mirror and then I went in my room. Right now, just telling you about this, I can feel the chair against my feet. I was so aware, probably more aware than I ever recall being before or after. The wood pressed against my bare feet, the rope thick in my hands. Sometimes when I'm in that strange moment where you begin to fall asleep, but when reality is still trying to hold on to you, I can hear the sound of the chair echo off the floor, falling over, and I remember it all. I remember everything I felt and saw."

"What did you see?" I ask.

"Nothing. There was no white light. There was no sudden regret, no moment when I would have given it all for more time to appreciate the little things. There was just more misery, more sadness, and more darkness that stretched on endlessly. Until the darkness was all." He pauses and closes his eyes before speaking again. "Then I woke up in a hospital bed, with a bunch of assholes standing around me, trying to label what was in my head. They had their go-to list of chemicals that would make me normal, their scientific names of disorders to explain why, when I pictured life, I saw nothing. I was there for months. When I left, I wasn't any different. They just titled me chronic and told me to keep telling someone my problems and popping my pills."

I unbuckle my seatbelt and lean over, not hugging him, but tightening my grip on his arm and resting my head against his shoulder.

"We're both a mess," he says, tilting his head down against mine. "I'm sorry. You don't need this, too."

Looking up at him, I know it's going to happen. I know it's a terrible idea, but I can't help it. The thought of his absence aches too much and I want to know he's real. I take my hand away from his arm and reach into his hair, pulling his head closer to mine until it's too late to change my mind. He freezes, though, before he meets my lips, and whispers, "Are you sure?"

I'm not sure. I'm terrified. I don't think I can have a boyfriend, not right now. I don't know what I want and I feel guilty because I want to kiss him so badly but I don't want to promise him things that aren't true. But with his warm breath so close to my face and the chill of the car at my back, I nod.

35.

"We should get going," he says. We've been sitting in the car for more than an hour. There was a lot of kissing, but that was it. It was *really* good kissing, which is messing with my brain too much. I've been with one guy – from kissing to everything else – and none of it was like the way Jack kisses me.

"We could."

He laughs. "You're never going to believe me, Lily, but I really didn't bring you out tonight for your birthday to sit on the side of the road and make out. Not that it's a bad thing."

"No, it isn't."

"It's not much further," he tells me and I settle back in on my side of the car, watching him. He's smiling. For a guy with so much pain in his life, it amazes me how happy he is right now. Of course, I catch myself smiling, too.

It's only about ten minutes down the road from where we were, but the place we stop is just a dirt lot and a faded wooden sign. Jack opens the door and this time, he runs around to get mine before I finish getting my seatbelt off.

"You don't need to open it," I say.

"You're right. I don't." He brings me against him and kisses me again. This time our bodies are close and I can feel the swirling in every part of me. He makes it hard to remember why I'm scared.

We head down the winding path and there's a loud cry from an owl. It's like I pictured on that one afternoon in the woods behind my house – and then I see it. The lake, with the sliver of the moon rippling on the water's surface. The trees, dead, but surrounding us. The owl cries again and I understand. I understand so much in this moment.

"This is…" I can't explain. I can't say it, because it was a stupid story. It meant nothing. I've told Jack pieces of my life and about Derek and my mom, although not in full, and the story of the trees was just a random story. A quiet night when I was babbling and there were no big or important issues surrounding us. It wasn't about fear or death or loss. It was just a story about hope – but he listened. And more, he made it come true.

"When I was growing up," he says, "I used to go outside in my yard, and eventually in my grandmother's yard, and I'd look up to space. The stars always intrigued me. Some of the light that we see when we look to the heavens has already died. That fact sort of inspired me when I was a kid, both before and after my mom's death. The idea that, millions of years after the light dies, it's just now being seen by someone? That's crazy."

I nod, but don't add anything. He continues.

"For eight years, I asked for a telescope for my birthday. Even after my mom was gone. I was young enough to still not understand. I just wanted to see the stars. I never got the telescope, of course. We couldn't afford it, and really, there were more important things than staring at dead light."

"There aren't, though," I say. "This is the most important, Jack. This..." But words minimize it. He knows and I know. I don't need to tell him everything about Derek, about my past or my fears, because it's not important to him. He cares about me despite those things. I've lived so deluded about what caring looks like, but there's no question that this is what people do when they care.

He holds me against him, his body warm but tense. I know he has something to say and I feel like I know what it is. I don't want him to say it. Not yet. I want to hear it, but not now. Not until other things fall into place, because I need to get that right to make this what it should be.

"Lily... Elinor... the girl who has a plan for everything."

"Don't say it," I plead. "Not tonight, Jack. I'm not ready. I want to be ready, but I don't want to lie to you."

"Okay. I won't," he agrees. "Not until you're ready."

The cold doesn't bother me while we sit by the lake, arms wrapped around our knees and talking. The conversation isn't important – school, favorite movies, things that are transient, but the night is massive overhead. The sky is full of nothing but stars and light and the water spills onto the shore, inching closer to us as we speak. I remember the rainy day with Derek, but in this moment, I recognize what he was for me. You can't love an idea. When you do, you love that vague concept more than the person. Derek was the only one who stayed in the rain, the one who didn't tell me I had to come inside. He was the idea of freedom, but he also fit into the plan. It was safe rebellion, a sort of hallucinatory imprisonment. He represented what I wanted, but he still kept me locked away. Like that afternoon camping, I believed I was out in the rain, but we never left the tent. We were still protected from anything outside of us.

Jack is none of these things. He's dangerous because he doesn't care about rules. But if Derek was the idea of rain, Jack is the rain itself. He's the risk of failure and hurt, but I trust him. I believe in this boy.

"I don't want to hurt you," I tell him. "But I'm scared and I think I need to get other things worked out. I think I need to do certain things – alone."

"I know. I figured. I just wanted you to have a happy birthday. Even if it's late."

When we leave, we don't touch, walking distant to avoid the kind of stupid moves we made earlier. I care for him, but I need to be whole, to be separate from another person, to define myself without someone else's standards as a guide. I hate walking away from him when we get back to school and I don't know if it's a terrible mistake.

"I'll see you around," he says by the elevators. There's no kiss, no hug, no affection, but it's not cruel. I know it hurts him, too, and I want to tell him I changed my mind, but I can't. I can't make this what it was with Derek – an idea that never had time to manifest into what it really was, but existed like a photograph's negative of what I had imagined. Jack deserves more than that. *I* deserve more than that.

In the room, I turn on my desk light and in the dim space, I find the card and box he gave me; I'd forgotten about them in the immensity of the night. *He just literally gave you the world you had imagined, a world you mentioned in one casual conversation, and you walked away.* But when I think of changing my mind, of running to his room, I know what comes next and my body grows weak at the thought of it. I catch the bile as it rises, thinking about someone touching me intimately, the effects of being used, of how much things change once you open yourself to someone in that way. No matter how much I want to believe it might be different, I'm not ready.

The card is a simple black and white photograph of a moon. It's blank on the inside, except for the note from Jack.

Happy Birthday, dear Lily. Go believe in your moon.

Inside the box is a bracelet – a simple silver band with one charm – a silver leaf. It's nothing fancy, but it's personal, like the card, like the whole night, and I start to cry. The tears rush out as I try to shut it all out, every memory of my mom, of Derek, of all my failures and mistakes, but once it begins, it's like living your entire life in high velocity and you know the inevitable crash is probably going to kill you.

36.

Kristen's surprised when she gets back and my side of the room is fully decorated. I spent all day cleaning and putting up some posters that were sitting in the lounge. One is a motivational quote with a mountain on it and the other is from a movie that came out years earlier, but they're something. And I ate a granola bar, so she's even more excited when she sees the wrapper in the trash.

"What happened this weekend?" she asks.

"Nothing."

"You're lying. But okay."

"Really. It was nothing. It was just a lot of things at once and a lot of thinking and I can't keep letting the wrong things matter. I need to stop this. I can't change what happened and I'm angry and hurt and it's not okay, but I'm not letting it ruin the future, too. If my past is all a lie, at least I can write my own future, right?" I ask.

She closes the door and opens her bag, pulling out a Milky Way bar. "Here. Eat this. We'll split it. And tell me everything."

"Do you just carry food in there all the time?"

"Yeah, mostly."

It feels good to tell her, to explain it, to talk about the memories I've kept and hear from someone else that things weren't what I believed them to be. It helps to have another person look at me and tell me that it wasn't my fault. Although I don't completely believe it and despite my fears about going home for Thanksgiving, the idea that there is a girl inside of me who could be what everyone else sees – everyone beyond my mom and Derek and the me of a year ago – keeps me hopeful.

"I really don't want to go home, but I have to," I admit. "I have to face it. But she's going to want to talk about him and my brother isn't going to listen and I'm sure he'll have his own version and it will all be my fault."

"Who cares?" she asks.

"What do you mean?"

"I mean, if you want to make it a big deal, I will be right there with you, but if you don't and you want it to die, I'll be there for that, too. But who cares at all about the people who won't? If they can't see through it, maybe you're better off away from it."

"She's my mom," I try to explain. "I know it's stupid and I get how it looks to you, but she's the only mom I have." Hearing the words makes me think of Jack, of how much he misses a woman who didn't care about him while she was alive, how angry he is at his father for taking her, even though she wasn't perfect. He loved her although she was so far from perfect.

"Have you talked to them about classes?"

Most of my professors have been great, but I missed a lot and it's unlikely I can finish the semester with anything higher than a 3.0. It's only one semester and I'm on scholarship, but I have next semester to improve and bring it up overall. Plus a couple of the professors said they'd back me if it came down to academic probation. But my professors aren't my mom – and a 3.0 might as well be failing everything.

"I haven't. I don't know what she'll be most upset about – Derek, my grades, or how fat I've gotten."

"Well, those are all stupid reasons, so whatever. If she's awful, you can stay with me for winter break. And my mom loves food."

Laughing, I take a bite of the Milky Way she gave me earlier, which is the second thing I've had today. I can't express it to Kristen, but I love her, because she has never lectured me. She's not stupid; she knows I'm not okay. But she hasn't given me a speech about self-esteem or therapy or health or anything. She just comes back to the dorm with food when I'm not at meals – or she sends one of the guys with food. When I don't eat it, she doesn't say a word, but she never stops. Her faith in me makes me grateful we were randomly placed together.

"I'm glad our forms were matched," I tell her.

"Right, because I carry chocolate in my purse."

"Exactly. I could have ended up with a roommate who carried nothing but tampons."

She laughs and opens her purse, taking out a roll of Mentos. "Worse, they could've carried, like, broccoli."

"The logic in this hypothetical feels flawed," I joke.

Popping half the Mentos into her mouth at once, she says around the mouthful of coated chewy candy, "Logic schmogic. Eat a Mento."

People act like life is a series of big moments, of the things that shape you and when you're sad or even when you're happy, it's all these huge and impactful memories that come to mind. But the best moments I've had since college started involved sitting on the frozen ground by the lake with Jack and this – eating Mentos with a girl who's only part of my life because someone grabbed two pieces of paper at the right time.

****

Jack keeps his word and I don't see him at all before Thanksgiving. Every day I look for him, hoping I can blame fate for his presence, that I can excuse my joy at seeing him as an accident, but he's never there. I know he works, that he has band practice, that his classes are on the other side of campus from mine usually, but if I tried a little harder, our paths would cross. It confuses me because I'm still not ready, but I miss him. I miss watching him try to smuggle soup in his coffee mug because he says sandwiches aren't healthy. I miss the way he rolls his eyes when I try to remember the name of the game he's playing. I miss the fact that talking to him feels comfortable and when I'm working on my homework, he's usually nearby. I miss having him sit so close to me but still leaving me my space.

Going home is hard. Since the night with Derek, I've refused to let the past in, trying to think of nothing but who I want to be and what I need to let go. But I know the weekend will be a challenge. It's only Tuesday night and while I'm waiting for my dad, I can't stop worrying. Anxiety makes me chew on my pen and I end up biting down too hard, spraying ink across my teeth, mouth, and shirt.

"Awesome," I mumble and grab another shirt and a towel. The bathroom is empty because most of the dorm is already empty. Dad had to work late, so it's after seven and everyone else has gone home until Sunday.

I run the water, waiting for it to heat up, staring at the blue that coats my smile. There are too many things to talk about this weekend, too many fears, and I just don't have the energy to have ink in my teeth.

"Oh, hey. I didn't know anyone was still here." The girl isn't familiar, but she clearly lives here, carrying her shower caddy and change of clothes towards the showers. I want to ask her where she's going for the next few days or why she isn't leaving if she's not, but it feels rude. I don't know her.

"I was just trying to clean myself off," I explain.

She comes over and rubs hand sanitizer into the towel, which is sopping wet but water isn't enough to get the ink out of my shirt. I'm in a black skirt, tights, and dress shoes, with a ratty Winnie the Pooh t-shirt. The shirt we're washing is white and I don't think anything will make the ink come out.

The girl keeps scrubbing, though, and gestures towards her caddy. She makes a cocktail of body wash, toothpaste, and shampoo and scrubs my shirt with the expert skill of someone who still knows how to hand wash clothes. "How do you know how to do this?" I ask.

"I'm the oldest. My brothers – they're twins and they're eight – don't have anyone to clean up after them. My dad passed away a few years ago, so I've gotten really good at keeping the house clean while my mom works."

"Does she miss you? While you're here?"

"I don't know. It's hard because they're in California and I can only go home twice a year. I miss them a lot, but she refused to hear it when I suggested going to school close to home. This was the best school and the best scholarship offer and she says they're surviving. But I haven't seen them since August."

"That must be tough."

She shrugs. "It is, but they're right. It's a good school and I can't stay there forever."

I look in the sink, where the water has gone deep blue. Pulling the shirt out, I hold it up; the stain is gone. "Wow. Thanks."

"Here," she says and she hands me a toothbrush, still in its package. "Always have a spare toothbrush. Guess it's a good thing I did."

"Lily," I say. "I mean, I'm Lily. And thanks. That came out weird."

"You're fine. Meghan." She goes to the shower, now that the ink is mostly gone. I brush my teeth and use part of the towel to wash the ink off my face. Everything is perfect – no sign of damage. Almost on cue, my phone buzzes.

"My dad's here," I say to the bathroom, but the water is already running in the shower and she won't hear me.

I run back to my room and change out of my Pooh shirt into another white dress shirt and grab my bags for the weekend. I realize as I run down the stairs that Meghan and I have lived near one another for three months now and I've never even see her before.

I've spent too much time living in some kind of suspended life. Going home is going to be very different this time.

37.

He has the nerve to show up on Wednesday morning. By the time I got home last night, everyone was tired and I didn't have to socialize, but I'm trying to pick at a corn muffin my mom ironically insists I eat despite her comments about my weight and I don't need to see him right now.

"I was surprised you didn't bring Lily home," my mom says. She's washing dishes. I don't know why – Jon and I both just got back last night and the house is spotless. No one has eaten. I have no idea where the dishes even came from. The kitchen smells like lemon dish soap, though, and it's interfering with my ability to eat this muffin. Every bite tastes like detergent.

"Oh, she didn't tell you?" *Please don't,* I think, but it's pointless. He does. "She broke up with me."

In movies, my mom would be so shocked she would drop the dish and we would all enjoy the slow motion shattering. Somehow it would be some heirloom, too, just to instill in the audience what a terrible person I am. None of that happens, of course. She scrubs harder and refuses to make eye contact instead.

"I see. Well, Lily, I imagine you have a good explanation for this?"

I stare at the mangled muffin. Do I sit here, with him so close, telling her what he did? Would she believe me? Would she care? I can still feel him fighting me, can still hear the words he used. How would he defend himself? Would he even bother?

My brother has his head in the fridge, rummaging for food, and he's oblivious. He's always oblivious. My dad had to work, so I'm trapped in this room with all of my nightmares and I have only a corn muffin and my version of the story to support me.

"It just wasn't working," I say. "We want different things and being away at different schools was hard." Generic. Vague. Acceptable.

"I guess you should have considered going to school with Derek after all," she tells me. "I thought you were stronger than that."

So many words fly through my brain – arguments of my strength. I've survived what he did. Survived a year in a relationship that was toxic because I was too naïve to know better. Most of all, I have survived her and she stands there, doubting my strength? But as the defense takes form on my lips, I see her cleaning the already clean plate, her hair in a perfect updo and her clothes starched and ironed, and I realize it doesn't matter. She won't understand, but that doesn't mean I need to wait for her approval.

"I'm going upstairs. I have some schoolwork to do," I say and I toss the uneaten muffin in the trash, spilling crumbs and not caring.

I can hear their voices downstairs while I work. She made him breakfast and they're eating, talking about school and complaining about how difficult I am. *I'm sure he was so heartbroken*, I think. *He probably had to sleep with ten people just to get over it.* I'm angry, but mostly that I wasted so much time. All of high school really. Imagining him as a decent person.

I hate that all of my firsts were his.

****

Abby came home from Europe and all she wants to do is shop. It's escape, though, so I agree to head out after Thanksgiving dinner to stand in lines so we can buy a car or something for a dollar. The afternoon was unbearable, listening to my mother's questions that all focused on how I had failed her by ending things with Derek. The only respite was talking about Jon's new girlfriend or her joy at the fact that I was "dieting." I ate three carrots and wanted to puke, but she chalked it up to a success.

"It's really cold," I complain. We've been standing here for three and a half hours. The store won't even open for another five.

"Why do people do this?" she asks.

"I don't know. I thought you wanted to."

She shrugs. "I wanted to come home and suck up the American-ness. It gets really depressing sometimes to be an outsider."

"So *this* is your idea of being American?"

"Where else can you get frostbite just to save twelve dollars on a laundry basket?"

"How is Europe anyway? Your texts are cryptic as hell."

Abby looks around at the mob that has been growing. Some of these people have chairs and small grills. "Do you want to go somewhere else?"

"It's after six on Thanksgiving. Is there somewhere else?"

"Let's go to the city," she says. "Come on. No one is expecting us until tomorrow afternoon when we're wiped out from shopping. Something has to be open in the city."

With the exception of my camping adventure, I had never done anything off schedule. But the last few months had changed a lot and I don't hesitate. "Yes."

"Yes?" she asks. "What the hell? That was easy."

"Tell me about Europe – and I'll tell you about school."

Inside the car, Abby programs coordinates for Rockefeller Center into the GPS. I can't imagine we'll find parking and I really can't believe she intends to drive all the way in, but I'm not saying a word. This isn't about planning. It's not about logic. There will be parking somewhere and that will be the place where we should spend the evening. It feels freeing to leave it up to fate.

"So, I've been having a lot of sex," she says.

"Shocking," I remark.

"It's been good, Lily. It was what I needed, because I missed you. I missed home. I felt like a weirdo, walking around in these places where I could barely ask what time it was, and I probably ended up asking what color my potato was instead. Yet I'd meet these guys... and we'd fuck. It was mindless and stupid, but I had fun and I forgot that I missed you."

"I am sure there are a number of things I could say or that you expect me to say, but I'm not. I missed you, too. And I'm glad you were at least distracted. Although I was kind of expecting you to tell me about crepes or something."

She laughs. "Sometimes, it's lonely, though. All the sex and all the museums and clubs and everything? I'm still alone every morning. Europe isn't a person. Random guys aren't friends. It's great, but it's not what I expected."

"Neither is college," I admit.

"They don't tell us anything. They just tell us to go be people, to go live a life, but after high school, there were no rules. I love it, but sometimes I just kind of wish someone would tell me what to do next."

"Are you going back for the spring? Or are you going to start school earlier?"

"Hell, no. I love it. Like I said, it's lonely, but I don't even know if I want to go to college at all. I don't think loneliness is tied to place. I've been thinking about why it's lonely, but it's because I tie it to some idea. I went to Europe thinking I would find myself or find my passion, maybe fall in love or something."

"But you haven't."

"I don't want to fall in love. A few guys have asked to spend the night, but I can't wait to get them out of my apartment. I had a long conversation with myself one afternoon-"

"While you were sitting along the Seine," I add.

"Shut up. No. I was in Florence actually. But it's not right, you know? They come to my apartment with no expectations, yet I should want more? Why? I have a great time for the night and then the next morning, I can get up when I want, can go where I want, and no one bothers me. I can stand in a museum and not have to explain a painting or wonder if the person I'm with is bored. I felt so selfish, but why should I? Why don't I have the right to be selfish? I think I'm pretty awesome. Of course I want to spend all my time with myself."

"I don't think it's selfish," I tell her.

"What about you? All you said is you and Derek broke up, but are you still waiting to be the perfect girl?"

"I don't think there's such a thing," I admit.

"What happened?"

"I don't know. I really don't know. When I got to school, I wanted nothing but to make things right. I wanted to do what my mom wanted, what Derek wanted. I don't know when it changed. Not really. But I started to feel like no one was listening. I made friends at school, but I couldn't shake the past, couldn't let go. On Columbus Day weekend, we all came home and Derek and I went to the hill and we had sex, as always, but I wasn't even dressed yet before he told me he wanted a break."

"He's such an asshole," she says.

I nod. "Yeah, I know that now. But I only kind of knew it even then. I went back to school and I was trying to move on, to let it go. He'd said he would visit after my birthday, though, so it was like I was on call for him."

"Probably so he could try out other girls to decide what he wanted." Although it's painful to hear it aloud, I know it's true and I thought the same things. It amazes me how she could see it so clearly for all this time and I couldn't.

"He came to my room one night and it was horrible. He was mean, Abby. Aggressive. He called me a slut and he held me down and I was afraid of him. Like honestly afraid."

"Did he...?"

"No, but the thought that he might? It was so obvious and I had never noticed."

Abby waits before responding. I know she probably has a lot of thoughts about Derek, since I don't think she ever really liked him, and she's my best friend so she's naturally angry, but she doesn't speak at first. I run my hand over the frost forming on the inside of my window while I wait for her to talk.

"I will do whatever you tell me to do," she finally says. "Even though every part of me wants to ruin his life, I will keep my mouth shut if you want to put it behind you."

"I do. I need to. I've spent too much time looking backwards."

"Okay. Then I won't say a word. We don't even have to talk about him ever again. What else is happening at school?"

I'll talk to her about Jack, but not yet. Instead we spend the drive on the easy things – classes for me, the places she's seen for her. For all of the things I have to leave behind to move forward, knowing Abby is heading in the same direction as me is a relief. You just can't ignore the value of having a friend who can meet you anywhere on your path and need no explanation.

****

Rockefeller Center is busy for nearly midnight on Thanksgiving. People are skating even though the rink is closing soon. Abby managed to find parking, which cost a small fortune and we're watching people below us, the wind weaving its way through the area but it's a lazy wind. The buildings keep out the strongest parts of it.

Music plays from speakers somewhere and I sit on a bench nearby, sharing it with a man and his daughter. Abby gets coffee for both of us from somewhere – she seems to know how to find coffee at any hour – and I hold it, keeping my hands warm but not drinking it. No one knows we're here, no one here knows us, and it might be a stupid tourist thing to do, but I don't care. I like the anonymous beauty of it.

Squeezing between me and the father, Abby settles herself and sips her coffee. "So tell me."

"Tell you what?"

"The part you're leaving out."

"How did you know?" I ask.

She looks at me sideways. "Seriously?"

"I don't know. It's so complicated. There's a guy."

"Isn't there always?"

"Yeah, that's the problem, right? I have all this other stuff and I don't know where to put this right now. I don't have a place for him."

"What's his name?"

"Jack," I say and I give her the quick version. I don't go into details about his past or his family life, although I do tell her that he has a lot of trouble at home. I briefly explain his situation with Alana, again leaving out the details that are hers, and I finish by describing the night by the lake. "It was perfect, you know? Just at the wrong time."

"Was it perfect? You've spent all this time telling yourself Derek was perfect and look at that. Don't be unfair to any chance this has to work out. It's not perfect, but that's okay. The real question is how do you feel?"

"I don't know. I'm starting to be comfortable. It's not only around him, but I never have to pretend with him. Maybe that's why he made me happy that night. I don't have to be anyone else."

"That's a good thing."

"But I don't want to move from one mess into something else. I shouldn't need him or want him. I should be independent."

Abby takes my coffee and stands up, waiting for me to follow. She hands it back to me after I stand up and we make our way down the street, with no plan or direction. As we turn the corner into a crowd, she says, "Stop thinking about what you should do and just do what you want."

We spend the night walking, taking breaks in coffee shops and diners, until it's morning and we head to Central Park. For Abby, this probably feels common. She's been places I've only imagined from pictures or books, but for me, for someone so obsessed with order, watching the sun slowly wake the city is more than symbolic. I'm still carrying the coffee cup, cold and empty now, like a last souvenir from how things were. All of these recognitions aren't world-changing; no one is going to start a movement about me and my broken hopes. But I stand, taking in the world as it begins what's just another day, and I do something I never have: I like myself.

38.

Suffering through the rest of the break with my mom is easier than I expected, because she seems to have decided I don't exist. She never listened in the first place, I suppose, but for once, I don't care. I spend the days locked upstairs in my room and head back to school on Sunday with everything caught up for school. This is the third time I've come back to my dorm – after moving in and the long weekend in October – and it's different. Instead of it being heading back to school, I feel like I'm coming home.

Kristen's back because her stuff is spread out over her bed and the light's on, but I don't see her. She and Lyle were introducing each other to their families this weekend, so I imagine they're having some kind of parental debriefing right now, followed by whatever else they feel like doing. I turn on music and unpack.

Abby's presents from Europe take up the majority of my extra bag.

My phone lights up and I reach over, assuming it's Abby to see if I made it back and to make plans. She's stuck at home and I promised she could come up to visit. It's not her, though, but Jack.

Happy Thanksgiving. It's been a while. No worries if you don't want to talk yet.

I do want to talk. I want to talk very much.

I missed you. Are you around?

Two minutes later, he knocks on my door. I'm smiling when I open it; it's cute that he was waiting.

"Hi," he says.

"Come in." I make room for him on my bed, pushing a box of macarons to the side. Half of Abby's presents are food-based.

"How was your break?" he asks.

"It was good. It was really good actually. What about you?"

He shrugs. "The same as every holiday."

"Was it just you and your grandmother?"

"No, just me. My grandmother goes to the prison to spend time with people there on the holidays. She feels like they're all alone and shouldn't be."

"But what about you? You're alone then?"

"She invites me. I just don't feel like being there. I'm not sure I'll ever be in a place where I feel bad about my dad being alone. He put himself there. I only visit him when she makes me feel bad about it, because it matters to her. I figure it's the least I can do, right?" He picks up my alarm clock and starts fidgeting with it. I'm not sure he knows he's doing it; it's a matter of distraction and reflex.

"I'm sorry. That's a crappy holiday."

"It's okay. Alana usually comes over and we usually end up spending it drunk. But her mom met someone and this one... I don't know. He actually seems like a decent guy so she's trying to get to know him. She's more forgiving than I am."

"I wish I'd known. I would've called or something."

"No, it's really okay. I did go see my mom – well, her grave. I mean, I go there every weekend, but I like spending time there. No one else goes anymore. Even my grandmother only goes once or twice a year."

269

"Wow."

I reach for the macarons and offer him one, not sure what to say. I kind of understand why people just shove food in your face every time you're sad. He takes it and his eyes land on the bracelet he gave me. I haven't taken it off since he gave it to me.

"I never said thank you. Not really," I apologize.

"You didn't have to. I'm glad you like it, though."

I take a bite from one of the other macarons and Jack and I watch each other in sugary silence. Kristen comes back in eventually, sees us, and then leaves with a bag of clothes, making up an excuse about needing to move her car. It's funny how comfortable I am around Jack and yet how nervous and awkward I feel right now.

"Do you want to go somewhere? Get dinner? Something?" he asks after Kristen leaves.

Packing up the macarons, I move the box to my dresser and clear space from my bed before leaning towards him. He watches me, his hands spread flat against his thighs. His hair, dark and too long, keeps getting in the way of his eyes. I don't know who reaches across the space first, but it's gone and his lips meet mine. The taste of the macaron is still on them, sweet and foreign and overwhelming.

"There are things I need to tell you," I say, "but I don't want to talk about them right now."

"I don't want... I mean, I didn't come over... You shouldn't think-"

"I don't think it. I am completely aware of what happens next, Jack. And yes, I am definitely sure I want it to happen."

This time, when he kisses me, the voice in my head doubting it is quiet. I lean back with Jack over me. I know where this goes and I'm okay with it. I want to go there, even if we haven't defined this or explained it. I know he cares and that's enough. He pauses and looks down at me.

"Lily, I-"

"I know. Me, too."

Although it's not new for either of us, everything about it feels new. He tells me I'm beautiful and I feel it when he looks at me. He doesn't have cheesy lines about sunsets, but his eyes and hands tell me the same thing. When before it felt like an invasion, now it's equal and it's amazing. None of the fears I had every other time are present; nothing is present but us and the moment.

With Derek, when it was over, it was just over. It happened and that was it and it felt like being abandoned each time. With Jack, it ends but not really. He holds me and I fall asleep with him. And he's there in the morning.

****

Abby comes up to visit a few weeks later, right before finals, and Jack has a show. I promised to cover it for the paper, which was my form of an apology for being MIA for a month. They hadn't even noticed.

Jack and I still haven't given anything between us a name. I spend most nights with him, and it feels like enough. But while Abby watches me try to get dressed for the show, everything feels wrong. I'm sitting in a pile of discarded clothing. Kristen gave up hours earlier and told me she would just see me at the show.

"I think I need you to help dress me," I tell Abby. It's the invitation she's been waiting for and she begins sorting through the piles and searching my closet.

"You literally do not own one sexy thing. I know your mom is nuts, but how did I let you go away to college looking like a pilgrim?"

"I think I have a tank top," I suggest.

"Hopeless."

She ends up finding an olive green dress in the back of my closet. It's a hideous thing I've never worn. I bought it because it was on sale and I thought it looked good on the mannequin, only to realize that I don't look like the mannequin. Grabbing a pair of scissors and a black sweater, Abby orders me to strip. I stand in the middle of my room in my underwear while she cuts up my clothes and swears about something. Finally, though, she stands up and comes over to me with the dress. I don't know what she did, but it looks fantastic. She somehow merged the dress and the sweater into one dress; it looks feminine and sexy and tough and it's absolutely perfect for tonight.

"Wow."

"Where am I staying tonight?" she asks.

"I don't know. I didn't really think about it. Here, I guess. I mean, I don't need to stay with him tonight."

"Yes, you do. You have less than ten days before the semester ends and I think you have some things to resolve. He's in love with you, you know," she says. She only met him briefly this afternoon at lunch, but I suppose our feelings aren't unclear.

"I do know. But neither of us has said it. It feels like... well, it's definite. And it scares me."

"I get it, but Lily, I was never a fan of Derek. I didn't like what he did to you and I didn't like how afraid you were to be an entire person with him. I don't think it's Jack that scares you, though."

"Then what is it?" I ask.

"I think you're terrified of being with someone who expects nothing, who truly loves you because you're you. I don't think you know how to live up to that."

I don't reply, digging through my closet to find shoes. I come up with a pair of black combat boots that I've had since high school, but also never worn. Abby thought they looked badass and we each bought a pair, but then we realized that we lived in a town where people only wore combat boots if they were in the military. I don't even know why I brought them with me to school, other than that maybe a part of me subconsciously envisioned college as a chance to reinvent myself. Regardless, I'm glad I did.

"I'm trying," I say, when I have the boots laced up and I'm ready to go. "I really am."

"I know you are. Still, one of these days you'll realize that the best people are the ones you don't even have to try with, Lily."

39.

It's hard to make it to the front; the club is packed. It's slightly bigger than the last venue where I saw them play, but there are more people now, too. They're also headlining this show. Jack says they're not any good, but after the opening band, even more people push towards the front.

"Lily, over here," Alana calls and she makes room for me and Abby. Kristen and Lyle are sitting on a couch in the back, but they're happily enjoying the music from there.

When they come on stage, and Jack is suddenly standing inches from me, I have to close my eyes. I need to tell him tonight, to explain what happened before, but also tell him how I feel about him. I know nothing about music, know very little about the band except that it's important to him, but when I open my eyes and look at him, the concert is just a thing. This is filler. I've never been around a person who makes someone else this significant in their life, but Jack makes me the center of his.

I don't move during the entire show. By the time it's over, the club is full of energy. Alana introduces Abby to Neil, the singer, whom I guess she knows through Jack. Everyone is talking, but I don't move. I stand in the same spot by the stage, waiting for him to come back.

"Elinor."

I kiss him in reply, my hands holding his at our sides. "I don't think so. Not anymore," I say when we move apart.

"Everyone wants to head out, to get something to eat. Do you want to come?" he asks.

"I do, but… did you bring your own car?"

"Yeah, do you want to ride with me?"

We make arrangements for Alana to take Abby, Kristen, and Lyle, and the four of them follow the band to the local diner. I tell Abby that we might be a little late and she just tells me to take my time.

"You ready?" Jack asks once the van is loaded with their equipment and everyone heads out. It's starting to snow, but not enough to stick on the roads. It's the perfect snow – light enough to make the world magical without interfering.

We drive for a while, holding hands but not talking. There is heaviness in telling him, even though I know he feels the same way. But Abby's right. Jack looks at me in a way I always wanted to be looked at – by my mom, Derek, people at school. He looks at me like I'm actually perfect and now that I've accepted it's an impossible standard, I'm afraid I'll disappoint him.

"Let's stop here," I suggest. It's a small playground and it looks like no one has been here in years. We walk to the swings after parking the car and Jack brushes off a clump of leaves so I can sit, before joining me on the other one. He digs the toes of his boots into the light layer of snow and dirt beneath him, drawing lines and patterns.

"I'm really glad you came tonight," he says. "You look beautiful."

"I need to tell you, about everything."

"Okay," he nods.

"It started with my mom. It was never enough, Jack. If I failed a test, I was a failure for life. I had a dog and..." I can't talk about Lucy without crying. The tears come before the words. I tell him the whole story, the rules, how easy it was in the spring and summer, but then the math class. I describe the running and how ashamed she was for peeing. "My mom sent her back because I screwed up, but Lucy looked at me like it was her fault. She thought it was because she peed, because she'd let me down. Jack, she was perfect, and I messed up. What if no one came for her? What if they needed to make room in the shelter and she was the unlucky one? All because I was too stupid not to make a mistake. What if...?" I can't finish. I hate it and it hurts to remember her.

He holds my hand and looks up at me. "That's horrible, but it's bullshit. You don't really still think it's your fault, do you?"

"Not exactly, but what if she died because of me?"

"She didn't."

"How do you know she didn't die?"

"I don't," he admits. "But I know it wasn't your fault. You can't be perfect. That's a ridiculous standard.

I'm sorry your mom can't see that, but no one can live up to that."

"I have to. She might have died because of me."

"God, Lily," he says, pulling my swing towards him and trying to hold me. It's almost impossible at this angle, but he tries anyway. "You can't never make a mistake. That's impossible."

"That's just it, though. I was supposed to – and I wasn't good enough."

"Good enough? Seriously? Let me tell you what you are, okay? You're a girl who cares about other people, even when you have your own shit to deal with. You met me, and you walked through my life, and never once did you comment on it or judge me or tell me it was too much. You trusted me to be your friend for no reason but because we had shitty coffee one night. Someone that open doesn't let people down, unless the people let down are incapable of being satisfied."

"It wasn't just her, though," I tell him. "For all of high school, I thought my life would be perfect if only Derek noticed me. If only he saw me as enough. He had been with most of the girls in school, had dated the most popular and most attractive and smartest and everything else, but he didn't even see me. I was right there in front of him, almost daily, and he never saw me. If I was invisible, if I couldn't live up to those girls, I was obviously nothing."

"I'm not arguing with you," he says. "Not because I agree, but because it makes me angry. I want you to tell me, but you need to realize I hate the guy."

"I know. And you should. *I* should, and I do in a lot of ways, but it's hard sometimes. The thing is when he finally paid attention, when he told me I was sexy and he wanted me, I was willing to do anything. And I did. I gave up everything and he never appreciated it. It was just something to do, someone to be with, but I wasn't any different than anyone else. Not for him.

'We had broken up when you and I became friends. But I still needed his approval, my mom's approval. But when he came to the dorm that night, when you fought, he made me feel worthless. In a way I didn't know how to accept."

Jack stands up and takes my hand, bringing me towards him. Brushing a hand across my cheek, he looks directly into my eyes. "Lily… I'm not a good guy.

I'm not really anything special. I'm sure your mom wouldn't approve."

"She wouldn't, but it's not that. I'm not trying to make a point," I argue.

"I know. I believe you. The thing is, if I ever make you feel worthless, which I don't intend to do, but if I do... I want you to tell me. I never want you to be silent."

"The night at the lake, you started to say something and I told you I wasn't ready."

"I love you, Lily. I am in love with you in a way I don't think I deserve to feel. But I do love you. I tried to tell you the night we... the night after Thanksgiving."

"I know. I told you I did, too, but I still couldn't say it. But I do, Jack. I do love you."

"I missed you a lot when you didn't want to see me," he says.

"It wasn't right. I didn't want to tell you, to be with you, unless I was sure. I didn't want this to be a replacement for something else that was broken. I wanted this to be my choice."

"And you're ready now? You're sure?" he asks.

I kiss him, the cold of the night an illusion. It's like living in a snow globe, where it's pretty and comfortable without any of the mess or damage of winter. He holds me in the playground, the moon peering through dusky grey swathes of cloud.

"I thought he was my future," I explain. "I thought there was nothing else, and that night, it hurt to see how blind I had been. It was like staring into an endless eternity and knowing that it was all hopeless. The world looked bleak and I didn't want to bring that into us. When you told me about your life, I felt like I should want to put you back together, to make it right, but when my own life shattered like that, I realized something. No one needs to put anything together. We're fine just like this. I want this... exactly as we are."

"Why? With all of the things that make me what I am? Why wouldn't you want to fix it?"

"Because those are the things that make you the guy I fell in love with."

"You really love me?" he asks.

"I do. I have for a while now. I didn't want to say it, didn't want to feel it, because I wasn't ready for it. I wanted to move on, to be myself separate from someone else. It was bad timing, but it didn't make it less true. I guess I thought, though, that if I moved on, if I didn't miss you, if I didn't yearn to see you every time I took a corner, then I would know."

I take his hand, heading back to the car. "Jack, it was your eyes I saw when I fell asleep at night," I say. "When I walked to the elevator every day before class and every afternoon after class, I waited for you to come through the doors, and every time you didn't, I ached for you. I looked for you every night when I ate dinner. Every voice I heard sounded like yours. I never felt like that with Derek, when I thought it was everything I had ever wanted, but I felt like it with you and I couldn't stop it. I don't know why. Something about you, something in you just makes sense for me."

"I know better than anyone what it feels like to be missing something. I don't want to rush you. I can wait. If you aren't ready."

"I'm still trying to find myself and figure myself out. It's not going to happen overnight and it'll be a long road. But I wouldn't mind the company," I say.

"Are you sure?"

"Yeah. It's the only thing I'm sure about," I tell him.

40.

"I expect you to work things out with Derek over break. This is getting ridiculous."

Three days. There are three days left of exams and then it's Christmas and break and she calls to tell me this. I listen to the message several times, waiting for it to change, waiting for her to say she's kidding. But she doesn't. She doesn't even mention Christmas or our plans or what I should get my dad. Just that I need to resolve things with a guy who sees me as nothing but trash.

Jack and I haven't talked about the holidays, about options. I can't imagine bringing him into my family, into the parade of questions, the passive aggressive comments that make you feel like you'll never be more than a mistake. But the alternatives are not seeing him at all or telling my mother I'm spending the holidays with him elsewhere. And neither of those feels likely.

"Who was that?" he asks. I've been playing the message over and over again and getting angrier. The doodles in my notebook have gone from flowers to big black scratches of fury.

"My mom."

"And?"

I don't want to tell him, because it will hurt him, but I don't want to lie, either. I just hand him the phone and let him listen to it.

"Well, then," he says.

"Maybe I shouldn't go home. Maybe I should apply to stay over break." We have students from other states or out of the country who live in one of the dorms for the few weeks. It's a bit of a process and I'd have to dig up the money, but it feels ideal right now.

"You have to go home. You won't feel okay if you don't."

"I'd rather spend the holidays with you."

He takes a carton of egg nog out of his fridge and pours some into a plastic cup. "Here. The holidays in my house. With less rum."

287

"That's depressing."

"That's the holidays," he replies.

"I'm spending Christmas with you." I make the decision here, but this is what I want. I don't want to sit around in my house and listen to my parents tear each apart, to listen to my mother praise Jon for the same things she condemns me for doing. I don't want Jack to spend Christmas alone or at his mother's grave by himself.

"That's a big step," he says.

"I don't want to spend it without you. I'm still going to have to deal with her eventually, so why ruin the holidays, too?"

"Will he be around? During break?"

"Derek?"

"Yeah," he confirms. "Is he going to show up?"

"Probably. He's always around. His parents are friendly with mine and he's spent so much time at my house over the years that he's almost like family. To *them*."

Jack puts the egg nog back in the fridge, his palm pushed hard against the door, and I watch his chest rising with the slow breaths he takes, the ones he uses to tell himself not to be angry.

"I know you want to hurt him," I say. "I know you don't want me to think that of you, but in this case, I want him hurt. I just don't want to drag you into a mess where you don't belong."

"I can't stand the thought of it, the idea of him trying it again."

"You trust me, right?"

He turns around. "Of course I trust you. Lily, I'm not worried about you seeing him and realizing you still have feelings for him. I just can't bear to think about him trying again. I know you don't want to say anything and I respect that and I won't tell you what to do. I just hate that he's walking around and he doesn't even know it's not okay."

"He won't. He won't touch me," I promise Jack.

"What about your mom?" he asks.

"I don't know. I really don't know what to do about her."

"If you need to stay longer… if you can't deal with it…"

"I know, but I'm tired of running away from it. You're right. I need to go home. I won't be okay with it otherwise. It'll just feel like hiding."

"It's just an option, okay?"

I drink my egg nog and hold out the cup, the milky white plastic coated in the creamy liquid. Reaching out, I draw along the lines with my pen, branching out until the black lines become a flower and then the flower becomes a garden. All on the cup and all connected.

"We have three days," I tell him. "Three days where they don't exist. I don't want to talk about them now. They've owned too much of my life."

"What do you want to do then?"

I pick up his game controller and turn on the system, sitting on the floor and leaning against his bed. "Teach me how to not suck at this."

He sits down beside me and reaches over to turn on the TV, before settling back in and putting his arm around me. "Lily, I have terrible news for you."

"Yeah? What's that?"

"You are simply unfixable when it comes to this."

"You told me I could do anything I wanted to." I mock pout.

"Okay, well, I lied. Anything but this. You are seriously, by far, the worst gamer I've ever seen."

"Movie then?" I ask.

We stay on the floor, watching a movie we've both seen several times just because it's on and we're too lazy to look for something else. It's distraction, but I'm happy in Jack's room, just sitting on the floor, sipping his egg nog and eating candy canes he manages to produce from nowhere. Not once does he kiss me or touch me beyond letting me lean against his arm, but I don't doubt that he would if I wanted it. It's a relief to be with someone who doesn't demand a thing.

****

On the last night of exams, and the day before we all have to go home, Lyle decides to throw another party. His "party" is him and Kristen and me and Jack, plus Kendra and Don and some other kids from our hall I've seen in passing. Paul's nowhere to be found; several people have already left for the break since their exams ended a few days earlier so I figure he's one of them.

"I didn't want to do pizza," Lyle says when we get there, revealing boxes of takeout chicken and sides from the diner. "But I don't think I planned this very well."

I'm trying to be better about eating, but there's too much food and the whole room is stiflingly warm and smells like chicken. "Thanks, but I'm okay for food."

"Lily, please. Eat some corn or something. I'm an idiot." He looks heartbroken that his plan was poorly executed and Kendra is coming in behind us with her roommate. I take a plate from Lyle and scoop up some corn before sitting on one of the plastic bins he flipped over for chairs. Jack sits beside me, his plate full of chicken and potatoes and some kind of weird beet thing.

"What is that?" I ask.

"I have no idea."

"Excellent. But you're gonna eat it still, of course."

"Of course." He takes a bite of it and swallows.

"Verdict?"

"It tastes a little like feet." I say nothing when he eats the rest of it.

"Everybody eat up," Lyle says. "I think I got too much."

"You got *all* of it. There are ten of us. Incidentally, that's probably a fire hazard or something," Don adds.

"We're watching Rudolph," Kristen announces and she leans over to turn on the TV and his Xbox, so she can stream the movie. It starts, too loud for the room, which is already full of noise, but with ten people talking, too quiet for anyone to actually hear it. The room's an endless buzz of voices and eating and Hermey dealing with his life issues. I think of the uncomfortable quiet that's waiting for me at my house, the silence between the comments my parents make to each other, the unspoken judgments my mother thinks loud enough for us to know they're there. I want to curl up in this room and bring this with me, to wrap myself in the *living* that exists here before I'm stuck in the vastness of failure again.

"Kristen, toss me a soda," I yell.

"Watch out," she says and she throws it over a couple people's heads. I still don't know their names. They're just people and college is full of people. I remember the first night, how lonely I felt in the cafeteria, but I know that tomorrow I'm going to crave this.

"What are you guys doing for New Year's?" one of the random people asks. It's not directed at anyone in particular.

"My parents have a big party every year," Kendra says, "and I'm looking forward to spending time with my sisters. Two are away at different schools and one's married, so it's one of the few times when we're all together."

"We're leaving for Florida tomorrow as soon as I get home," Lyle says. "We always spend Christmas and New Year's down there with my grandparents."

People go through their plans – parties, work, quiet nights in with friends or family – and I listen, trying to imagine other people's lives. It's like when you're driving late at night, and there are only a few houses with lights on. You can't help but wonder about the people inside. Are they having trouble sleeping? Maybe they're night owls? Maybe they just got home from work? It always feels like when you try, though, you find yourself inserting your own story into their lives. It's hard to truly see things as someone else.

"You're quiet tonight," Kristen says, pulling up her own bin. Rudolph is still doing his reindeer thing, but no one is paying attention anymore. Someone put on Christmas carols, too, so it's just noise.

"I'm just going to miss this." She looks over at Jack, who's been drawn in to the struggles of the Island of Misfit Toys apparently. I follow Kristen's eyes and then turn back to her. "Well, yeah, of course, but not just him, not just us. I'm going to miss all of it. I feel normal here."

"It's only a few weeks."

"I guess."

"Seriously, Lily, I wasn't kidding when I said you could come stay with me."

"I know, and Jack offered, too. I could probably stay with Abby, if it came down to that, but I feel like I need to try, you know? I need to see it, to see if it's fixable."

"And if it isn't?"

"I don't know," I admit. "I haven't really thought that far ahead. I just don't want to quit without trying."

"Are you and Jack doing something for Christmas?"

I nod. "I already told him I'm spending it with him. Now, breaking it to my mom..."

"It's only a few days, and then it's Christmas, and if things are tough, come stay with me for New Year's. Just for the day, to break it up. It'll go by fast, but if it doesn't, you have options."

"I think I'll be okay. But... I really appreciate it. Because I think even knowing they exist makes it easier."

Maybe these are things I should have known from the start – that people exist who respect you for who you are, that it's okay to make a mistake, that you can care for another person without needing them to fit your own standards. Maybe it shouldn't have been hard to figure out, but it was, and I can't picture what a month at home will do. Although I don't say it to Kristen or Jack or anyone, I'm terrified that I'm still the weak girl whose mother will never be happy, who hides herself to make someone like her, who can't speak unless the words are written out for her on paper. But I know I have to find out. I know I can't just hide out and pretend anymore, and that gives me a little hope.

41.

On my first night at home, Jon invites Derek to stay over. I stand in my doorway, needing to pee, but he's in the bathroom. I don't want to look at him, don't want to be near him, don't want to remember how it felt to be close to him. People say time heals things, but time has only allowed me to put it away in my mind. Being here, with him in the next room, though, reminds me of so many things. The nights they'd come back from school and Derek would sneak into my bedroom, spending an hour or two with me doing what he wanted before leaving me, so I woke up alone. It was always the same story – he didn't want anyone to find us together. Now I remember being vulnerable with him, his hands on me, his knowledge of the most intimate parts of me, and then I remember the last night with him.

I can't bear to see him, can't imagine what he would say. I'm wearing my favorite pajama pants, blue and green fleece, and he's had his hands on them, in them. He's pulled them off of me before we had sex, and they feel like fire on my skin now. Burning memories of how weak I was, of all the times I wanted to say no, of all the things he never asked. I don't have a right to be angry; it was my fault for not speaking up. But I can't look at him and I close my door until I hear him making his way to Jon's room.

In the bathroom, after I pee, I sit inside in the bathtub, the coolness of it a cocoon. How can my family be so clueless? How can my *brother* not see it? I lie in the tub, wanting the comfort of school, of working on homework with Jack, of Kristen's endless candy supply, of things that don't make me feel guilty for living.

I can hear them talking, and I don't want to but I can't stop myself from standing in the hallway and listening. What does he tell my brother? What does Jon think of me? We haven't talked in years, so what version of me exists for him?

"It's not like you wanted to leave," Jon says. They're so loud. My parents are sleeping, but they're only on the other end of the hall. Jon's door is partly open. I wonder if my parents hear the stories and just pretend, or if they really don't care about anything we do.

"I didn't say that. I just said you had no problem taking off."

"You know I've spent all semester trying. I mean, Dianna McGillvery. C'mon. Give me a break."

"Yeah, she's hot and I get it. It sucked, though. Nothing happened and not for lack of trying."

"When we left, you were all over Caitlin Barnes. It didn't look like nothing," Jon argues.

"Man, she was all, 'but I'm still a virgin.' Did you see what she was wearing? And she *wasn't* there looking to hook up?" Derek asks.

He makes me sick. Everything about him makes me sick. These are the same conversations they had when they were sophomores in high school. Back then, I was naïve, stupid. I thought it was just how guys were, that it was big talk but no action, but after being with Derek, I want to hurt him.

"I thought you went home with her," Jon says.

"Well, yeah, she took some convincing, though. What a pain in the ass. It wasn't even any good."

My brother laughs, while I want to cry for Caitlin Barnes. I don't really know what happened. I don't know if she really did change her mind, or if Derek changed her mind for her. But I remember all the stories in high school, all the girls like Miranda Elliot, the ones who were angry at him, angry at me when I started dating him. I think about all of them and I head to my room. I could text Abby, Kristen, Jack, Alana... anyone. I could walk into Jon's room and tell my brother what Derek did. I could tell my parents. But I don't. Because tonight, Caitlin Barnes is sitting in her house, with her family, and I don't know what she's feeling. But if she's anything like me at all, I have an idea.

****

Two days before Christmas, after midnight in a small town, the police station is nearly silent. Radios spurt their news and updates periodically and somewhere, a machine – fax or copier – whirrs to life, but mostly it's dark and lifeless. The guy sitting at the front desk is barely twenty, his sandy hair only recently trimmed to what's likely police standard, and his uniform still out-of-the-packaging starched.

"I need to talk to someone," I tell him.

He puts down his book, because there isn't much else to do right now, and looks up at me. I wonder about people like him, people who have kind eyes, and if a job like this will change them. "What can I help with?"

"My boyfriend... no, my *ex*-boyfriend... I know there's nothing you'll be able to do, but someone needs to know."

"Are you reporting a crime?" he asks, reaching for a clipboard. I'm sure it's procedure, that it's the way these things are typically handled, but it's so cold to have people put down all their fears and experiences on paper with a pen hanging from a dirty string.

"I'm not sure. I don't know if it is a crime."

I can see him debating, because he doesn't want to ask. He doesn't want to say the wrong thing, probably partly because he's worried that someone will claim he pushed me into reporting.

"Would you like to meet with someone on duty?" he asks.

"That might be better."

I sit on one of the benches in the lobby while he goes to find a detective. I didn't bring my phone inside; it's sitting in the cup holder in the car because I was afraid I'd text someone and they'd want to come, to help me, to walk me through it, but I need to do this by myself. I need to tell them *my* version and not have it filtered through someone else, even if they mean well.

The waiting feels endless, but the clicking of the clock as it passes each minute argues otherwise. The man who comes out to talk to me arrives in less than nine clicks, which is probably good turnaround. Not that I really know.

"How are you doing, Miss...?"

"Drummond, but just call me Lily. This is all too formal already."

"Okay, Lily. I'm Detective Walker, but you can call me Sam, if you would feel more comfortable. We're just going to go into one of the rooms here, if that's okay? Do you want Chase to get you something to drink? Coffee? Water?"

"Water would be good," I reply and Chase, the blond guy from the desk, goes to grab it. Chase seems like an appropriate name for a cop.

When I have water, Sam leads me into a room that's more lifeless than the lobby even. It's not like those ones in movies with the double-sided windows. There's a window out to the street and a few file cabinets, as well as a coffee pot in the corner, but it's not a place anyone would want to be. Sam gestures towards one of the chairs and I sit while he gets out a folder and notepad to write down what I tell him.

"Before we start, Lily, I do need to ask you: Are you safe? Are you in need of medical attention?"

"No, it wasn't... I mean, it's been a while."

"Okay, whenever you're ready."

"Maybe I'm overreacting. Maybe this is stupid," I say.

Sam puts down the notepad. "Are you in school?" he asks.

"Yeah, Bristol University. I just started this fall. Why?"

"Just wondering. What's your major?"

"English. My mom still doesn't know. I applied undeclared, because she wants me to be responsible. She says sitting around reading books is for people who are too stupid to live in reality, that there's nothing useful about imagination. I told her I was considering economics, but at orientation... I love books. I love stories, and I just wrote it down. They told us we could change it anytime and if we still didn't know, we should just write down the thing that was closest to our passions. So I wrote it down and, well, I don't want to change it. So I'll tell her eventually, I guess."

"It sounds like your mom has pretty high standards for you."

"She does. Always. I guess it's why I didn't want to say anything, you know? I mean, it's my problem, not yours. Not anyone's. And she really likes Derek."

Sam picks up his pen again. "Is Derek your boyfriend?" It's obvious what he's doing, but I don't care. I want to tell him. I just needed to know how.

I shake my head. "No, my boyfriend's a few hours away. I met him at school. Derek's my ex."

"You mentioned to Chase that this was about Derek, right?" he asks.

"Yeah, Derek was my boyfriend for a year. Almost. Just under a year. We both grew up here."

"How long have you known Derek?"

"Most of my life. He's my brother's best friend."

"Older or younger brother?"

"Jon. Older, by 16 months."

"How did Jon feel about you and Derek?" Sam asks.

I shrug, thinking about Jon. He's never said anything. I don't know when it happened, not really. He was my knight in shining armor, my protector against the trolls in the woods, and then, a year or two later, he wanted nothing to do with me. "I don't know. We're not close at all."

"Does he go to Bristol, too?"

"No, he and Derek both go to Eastern."

"So what happened with Derek, Lily?"

Sighing, I reach for my water. The lights in this room feel too bright for this story, glaring at me like they're waiting for me to say the words, like they're judging me. *You're overreacting. You're going to make a mess of everything. He didn't do anything you didn't encourage. You're a fool.* "I thought I loved him. I really did. I wanted to make him happy. I'd liked him since I was a kid, and when he told me I was sexy and that he wanted to... well, I didn't know if it was a one-time offer and I thought I'd regret it."

"When was this?" Sam asks, flipping the page on his notepad. I wonder what kinds of things they write down. Do they really keep it factual? Is he just pretending anything I say matters?

"When we started dating, but that's not why I'm here. I chose it, even if I wasn't ready, but that's on me. I'm not blaming him. He could've done a lot of things differently, but he didn't force it. Not really. I wanted him to like me and I did what I thought would make him like me."

"So you and Derek had a sexual relationship?" I nod. "Was it... would you say it was frequent?"

"I mean, I don't know. We had sex every time we were together. He only came home every few weeks, but we never didn't have sex, if that's what you're asking."

"And when you did, was it always consensual?"

The lights flicker and it's like they're laughing at me. *No one's going to believe you.* "It was."

Sam pauses, flicking his pen a few times, and sighs. "Lily, I'm going to have to ask you things that may make you uncomfortable."

"He never raped me. Nothing like that. But the last time we were together... We'd broken up and he surprised me. He drove up to campus and I wasn't expecting him. He had asked for a break and I think I was starting to be okay with it, starting to maybe see things about him that I didn't like."

"Such as?"

"He was controlling. He never listened. He thought I was childish. Nothing really important, I know, but I'd started to see it. So when he showed up..."

"This was after you broke up, right?"

"Sort of. I mean, we hadn't really broken up, I guess. He wanted a break, but he told me we were still together. Just on a break."

"You were still dating him, but he was single, I suppose?" Sam asks, trying to make it sound reasonable, but hearing it all now just makes it sound even worse.

"I guess. So he showed up, but I was trying to be over it. And the second we were alone, he started touching me. He hadn't said anything to me except that he wanted a break and that I was needy and annoying and then he just showed up, wanting sex. I said no. I told him to leave, but he got mad."

Sam's writing it all down, but I realize there's nothing he can do. Derek didn't actually hurt me. He was an asshole and he made me uncomfortable and it's not okay, but he didn't technically do anything that the cops can deal with. I came here because of Caitlin Barnes, but I can't report something I don't even know happened.

"You can't do anything," I say. "He stopped. He scared me and he was aggressive and he called me names, held me down, whatever. But he stopped. I begged him to stop – and he did. I'm sorry I wasted your time."

"When did all this happen, Lily?"

"October 26."

"So nearly two months ago," Sam confirms.

"Yeah. I told you – I'm sorry I wasted your time."

"Why now?"

"What do you mean?"

"Why did you come to us now? Why not before?"

"It was my fault. I didn't want to upset anyone. I felt sick and I couldn't leave my room. But it was my fault. He was only there because I'd slept with him before, I'd never said no before."

"And tonight?"

"He's at my house. My family doesn't care. They're mad at me for breaking up with him. I heard him talking and he said he was at a party and there was a girl... he said she took 'convincing.' I don't know. Maybe it was nothing, but what if she... I just don't want to find out that he didn't stop one day, and if I'd said something..."

Sam closes his notepad and leans back in his chair. He looks at me with the expression I wish I'd seen even once on my father – care, worry, and the desire to protect. I wonder if Sam has a daughter.

"I'm going to be honest with you," he starts.

"I know you can't do anything."

"We're going to talk to him, to get a statement from him. Based on that, you can decide if you want to press charges, how far you want to take it. In these cases, you're right – we often can't do much. Not because we don't want to, but it's hard to prove. You had a previous relationship. He'd broken up with you. He could claim you're saying this because you want revenge for him breaking it off."

"Why would I do that?" I ask.

"I'm not saying you would. I just want you to know what kinds of things people say."

"They'll say it's my fault. I know."

"It's not, Lily. There's no physical evidence, because he stopped, but what he did isn't okay. You can press charges, but chances are it'll be a long process and I don't know what you want to achieve, and a large part of me wants to tell you to go for it. But I also want you to know. It'll be news in town, maybe even outside of town. They'll dig up everything about you, everything they can use. You said you have a boyfriend now?"

I nod. "Jack."

"I apologize for asking, but have you slept with him?"

"I have."

"It will come up."

"You think I should just let it go?" I ask.

"No. I don't. I'm just preparing you."

"I don't want to have him arrested. I'm not pressing charges. I want it to die, to go away. I don't want my life to be on hold for him. I just want him to know I didn't forget. I want someone to know what kind of person he is… If he does it again and I didn't tell you… Will it be kept somewhere?"

"Like I said, we'll follow up. I want you to consider your options. I don't want you to say you don't want to press charges yet, because you've given yourself that route by coming here tonight."

"Who's going to know I came here?"

"We'll try to keep it between you and Derek, but I can't promise anything. We'll meet with him at his house."

"I understand."

"You're not going to hear this from many people, especially if you decide to press charges. But coming here? No matter what people tell you, Lily, this is a hard choice to make and I think you should know that. There are a lot of girls who don't."

"I just don't want him to do it again," I say.

We wrap up the interview and Sam walks me to my car. It's the middle of the night and it snowed while I was inside. I dread the morning, of what comes next once Derek knows I was here, of what happens if my mother finds out.

"I have a daughter," Sam says as he finishes helping me clear my windshield. "She's nine. If anyone ever..." He doesn't finish, shaking his head, and walking back into the station.

42.

I'm trying to get up the nerve to go downstairs. I can hear my grandparents admiring the decorations and my aunt is asking Jon about school. My mother ironed my clothes this morning and I watched her silently, thinking about my night and wondering if Derek would tell anyone. She's not speaking to me already, because I told her I plan on spending tomorrow with Jack, but it's Christmas Eve and we have company and it's on me to be social. I send Jack a quick text telling him I miss him and check my clothes one more time.

"Lily, you look so pretty," my grandmother says when I make it downstairs. "Are you still seeing that boy?"

"No, I-"

"She thinks she's too good for him," my mom interjects. "Went away to college and she's better than everyone." With her comment securely in place, she goes off to make sure my brother cleaned his room or something.

"We broke up," I tell my grandmother. "I met someone else, but he's not why. It just kind of happened."

"I'm sure he's a nice boy," she says. "And I'm sure you made the right choice."

"Thanks." I reach for a paper plate, loading it with snacks, although I'm not hungry. Food is a weapon in gatherings like this. Get asked too many questions and stick a meatball in your mouth to avoid them.

It's only a few hours, I remind myself. There are enough people here to make me invisible and my mother doesn't have time to focus on me. *What about the next month?* I ask my inner voice, but this time, conveniently, it has no reply.

While everyone is distracted, I make my way to the living room, hoping to get a few moments of peace. I've barely put down my plate, though, before Jon sits beside me on the couch and turns on the TV. There's nothing on, but he flips through the channels anyway. I almost tell him to just pick something, to stop the flashing stream of noise and images, but the doorbell rings before I can. I don't know whom we're still expecting, but the door opening and the noise of greetings float in from the other room while my brother continues his flipping.

I knew it would come, and the fact that it happens this fast is probably better. Get it over with and all that. But hearing his voice, listening to my mother invite him to eat something, hearing him say he just needs to talk to me...

My mouth is dry when he enters the room, my tongue sticking to my teeth when I try to pretend this is a casual visit.

"Can we talk?" he asks.

"Start talking."

"I'd prefer to go somewhere less crowded."

"I can leave," Jon offers, abandoning me in the living room with Derek, while everyone stands in the hall beyond. I don't want to go any further, though.

"I said everything I had to with the cops," I tell him.

"Why would you say that about me, Lily? You wanted it. You were desperate for it for years."

"Don't put this on me."

He comes closer, but I stay sitting. I won't let him intimidate me.

"Do you realize how much you screwed things up? My parents are pissed," he says.

"Maybe you should've listened."

"I stopped. I didn't do anything to you."

"You're kidding, right?" I finally look up at him, make eye contact. If we weren't in my house, around other people, he wouldn't hesitate to hurt me. "You made me feel obligated. You knew I was nervous, that I didn't want to, that I wasn't okay with it. What about Prom, Derek? What about the things you made me do, the things you told me you'd leave me if I didn't do?"

"You did them, Lily. Stop pretending you're not a slut just because you want your new boyfriend to think better of you."

"You really think that's what this is about?" I ask.

"Well, why now?"

"Because you can't do this, Derek. You can't just take and demand and get away with it. You don't have

316

the right to make anyone feel the way you made me feel, and I wanted to make sure you know that. I wanted you to know that if it happens again, people will know what kind of person you are."

He sits on the couch with me and I lean away from him, but he reaches out and grips my arm, digging his fingers in hard. His voice is a whisper, but the threat isn't quiet. "Listen, bitch, you're nothing and if you pursue this, I swear I will ruin you."

"I'm not pursuing it," I tell him. "But if you ever threaten me again, if you ever even look at me again, I swear to God, I will. You can ruin me all you like, Derek, because if you ever try anything like this again, I won't be quiet next time."

"This is your idea of quiet? I had to defend myself to cops on Christmas Eve."

"Maybe you should learn to listen a little better then. Now get your fucking hands off of me."

After he gets up, I try to let the nausea fade. I didn't want him to see it, to know it hurt, but once his voice is only an echo in the hallway, I pull my knees up to myself and try to breathe slowly. A year. I gave him a year of my life, and that's only if I don't think of all the time I wasted thinking about him. How does a person spend this much time not seeing?

"Lily, did you see Derek?" my mom asks from the doorway. "I invited him for dinner, but he said you wouldn't want him to stay. Why would you say that? Derek's-"

"No, Mom, he's not. He's not at all," I say. I don't know what I expect – maybe for her to see the tears I can't keep back and to recognize them as important? Maybe for her to listen to me, to ask what happened, to try not to judge? I just want something to happen besides more of the same.

"I don't understand why you can't behave. Derek's a nice boy and you're being ridiculous."

The dizziness is like a waterfall, spilling over me as I stand. *Do not show weakness to her*, I tell myself. I won't fall over. I won't let her bother me. I make it to the doorway where she stands before looking up. She stares at me and there's nothing behind her gaze. She's empty; my mother is empty. I could stand here for a hundred years and she would never see it.

****

I swore I wouldn't run away, but it's Christmas Eve and I'm sitting at Abby's in tears. I told my mom everything, right there in the living room, and she just walked away, telling me to get out if I was going to ruin everything. I can't care. I can't let her do this anymore. I wish this were a movie and we would have a big reconciliation and she'd hug me and tell me she loved me, but my life isn't the place for those things. As far as she's concerned, not only did I fail, but I also caused problems. When I stood in the doorway and tried to say goodbye to my father, who just looked sad as I left, she told me that if I pursued this with Derek, I could find another place to live for good.

"What can I do?" Abby asks.

I shake my head. "Nothing. Thanks for letting me wait here. Jack should be here soon." I texted him right away, but I didn't tell him why. I just asked him to come and he's on his way to get me.

"I'm glad you went," she says.

"To the cops?"

"Yeah. I know you're not sure, but even if you do let it go, people know. *Someone* knows, Lily. It makes it not your problem anymore. And he'll always know it's there. It's not going to go away and maybe he'll think next time."

"Maybe." I suppose this should feel like a victory, but it just feels like my boyfriend was an asshole and my mom hates me. I don't regret going to the police; I only regret that it happened at all. "She just stared at me, Abby. She looked right through me and all she was worried about was that I messed up her plans. What the hell is wrong with her?"

"Oh, Jesus, Lily. Short or long list?"

At least it makes me laugh. It's an ironic and somewhat depressing laugh, but it's still a laugh. Nineteen years – and most of them spent trying to please someone who is incapable of being pleased. My best friend has been here for more than half of those years and she's seen it all, but she never pushed. There are likely people who would be upset with Abby, mad that she knew and she didn't force me to face it, but I'm not. I wasn't ready to see it and I would've lost her, too. I would've shut her out because I didn't want to know.

"I'm lucky I've got you to put up with my crap," I tell her.

"I'm your friend. It comes with the territory. And now, it's Christmas Eve and your super amazing boyfriend is on his way and your mom and that asshat, Derek, aren't going to ruin even one more second of your life, okay?"

I nod, wiping the tears away, knowing it's not that simple, but wanting it to be. Even for one night. I could have yelled at my mom, could have made a scene, could have told her everything she was, but it was energy I would have exerted on someone with no substance. Abby's right; they don't warrant that kind of effort.

"Abby? Lily? Do you want some ham?" her mom calls up to us. They've been waiting to eat, waiting for me, because I came over and interrupted their night.

"Sorry about messing up your dinner," I say to Abby after she yells back that we'll be right down.

"There are three of us, and a ham. It can wait. Don't be ridiculous."

I don't want to eat their food, but Abby's mom insists and fills a plate full of ham and potatoes for me. She doesn't ask what happened, and Abby's dad just asks about school and my classes and everyone pretends this is perfectly normal, that there's always some sad, broken girl sitting at the table on the holidays. I easily slip into their reality, though, and it feels healthy to tell them about what I've been reading and the paper and Kristen and Lyle. So healthy that I don't see the lights in the driveway, don't register the knock on the door.

Jon stands on the steps, segmented by the screen door, which my mom would say should have been swapped out by now for a storm door, and slowly gathering snow. The white flurries spin under the porch light.

"What are you doing here?" I ask from the other side of the screen. Abby's parents take their food and go somewhere else and she tells me she'll be upstairs if I need her.

"I heard what you told Mom."

"Look, I know. I'm a failure, right? How dare I say anything about poor, perfect Derek, when it's my own fault he didn't want me. It's Christmas Eve and I'm not coming home, not now and maybe not ever, and I don't want to hear it, Jon. I don't want to listen to your excuses and I'm not going to stand there and have her blame me."

"I don't..." He pauses and flicks the snow off his shoulders and shakes it from his hair. "I should have known. He's a dick, but who cares? He was just my friend. And when you started dating him, it was weird and I didn't know how I felt about it, because I knew what he was like, but you were happy. I thought you were happy with him."

"How many times did he cheat on me at school?" I ask.

"I don't know. There was one time, right after we came home for your birthday, and he didn't come back to the dorm all night. I asked him, and he told me he had to deal with some things, and I didn't want to get involved. It wasn't my business, Lily. You were old enough to decide and we weren't close. I couldn't just start dictating how things should be for you."

"So why are you here?"

"I'm sorry. I let you down. And I just wanted you to know that I believe you."

I open the door and step outside, sharing the small space on the steps with my older brother. It's been years since we've even looked at one another and the tiny step is still a lot of space to cross. "I don't know if it's that easy," I admit.

He nods. "I know. But I just didn't want you to leave like this. I promised you, a long time ago, that I'd look out for you. I haven't, and I'm sorry. It was easier to stay under Mom's radar when she was always focused on you and I let you deal with it all. And Derek... I should have been there."

"It's over now. You weren't, but this isn't on you. And maybe, when things settle a bit, maybe we can get coffee or something. Catch up. Get to know each other."

"I'd like that."

"Yeah, me, too." I brush the newly accumulated snow off his shoulder, but we don't hug. After a few more minutes of awkward silence, he wishes me a Merry Christmas and leaves. I don't head in right away, watching the car until it disappears at the end of the road.

43.

It's funny that we're standing by another lake. The night is quiet, though, because the snow has driven everyone inside.

"How do you feel about it?" Jack asks.

"Good. I really do. Sure, there are things I wish were different, but I'm not staying there, and I'm not going to sit back and be silent. I've been that girl for too long."

Maybe I change my mind and I call my mother tomorrow. Maybe I call her in a week, or a year. Maybe I never call. After a few days, I might decide to stay with Kristen instead, or come back here with Abby. I don't want to start my relationship with Jack this way – needing him – but right now, it works. If that changes, there are other options. The greatest comfort, though, is that any choice I make, any decision, is mine. Entirely. If it's a mistake, I own it, but I think I'm okay with that.

"I never told you about the trees," I say. "That night – I told you about my imagination, about the lake and the moon, but I said I'd realized something about the trees, and I didn't tell you. It sounded stupid in my head and I didn't want to try to explain it."

"You can tell me now."

"Well, it's… You know how things have been, right? There was nothing more terrifying than change, because change meant learning the rules all over again, and if I already couldn't stop screwing up…"

He reaches for my hand and brings me close to him, standing behind me and wrapping his arms tight around me. The snow barely touches me when he holds me like this, landing on him instead. "I hate when you say that."

"Say what?"

"It's not screwing up to be someone, Lily."

"Yeah, I'm starting to get that now, but then… Anyway, I was in the woods and I was thinking about how much things change, about how they were so different, about how I was different. Most nights, I would fall asleep, so scared of waking up the next day and finding out that things had changed, of not knowing what to do next and making a mistake.

"There were only about eight leaves left on the trees. They were basically bare, and I didn't really even see them. But while I was standing there, thinking about change, one fell. It was just a leaf, brown from the snow and cold. I was looking up and it floated down over me, perfectly lined up for me to catch it. I did, and it probably sounds ridiculous, but it made sense, Jack. The trees change every year, right? Every winter, they die, and then they start over in the spring. And they're still beautiful.

"I'd known it that day, but it took me another year to understand. That's it, though, isn't it? We celebrate their changing."

I step away from Jack so I can face him. It's too dark to see his features in the shade of what's left of the trees. "I'm still scared of making the wrong choices," I admit.

"The only thing that matters is making them," he says.

In a life of blank pages, the story doesn't fill itself in overnight. It's not about getting the right words and putting them together, just so they can fit where the emptiness lays. Once the pages are turned, they remain empty, and covering the ones that follow won't change that. But for every new blank page, there exists a new photograph, a new memory, and a new story to tell.

Reaching my hand up to move Jack's hair from his eyes, I try to remember his face right now. The way he looks tonight, because tonight is just one page, one memory.

Someday, he won't look the same. Someday, it will be sunny or we might have argued or he'll have slept poorly the night before. Someday, I won't care about something my mother said. Someday, Jack and I will be different people and maybe we'll still love each other with all our imperfections, or maybe we won't. Someday, I will look back at this night, at this girl, and I won't remember how I was her, either. All of these somedays are alternate realities right now, but they're sitting alongside all the possible ways our lives could go, an endless and vast series of opportunities and concepts.

I don't know which one of those somedays will fill our story, will make up next week or next year. I don't know who I will be the next time I stand by this lake, when spring comes and the trees change again. I don't know what tomorrow will look like, but I really, really cannot wait to find out.

About the Author

Sarah Daltry writes YA fiction, plays too many video games, obsesses over British TV, loves animals, and has a sarcastic remark for anything. She's also a recluse who's likely nearly transparent given how little she leaves the house. You can find her online at http://sarahdaltry.com.